POLLYANNA
TO READ ALOUD

Adapted and abridged by OSCAR WEIGLE
from the story by ELEANOR H. PORTER

Illustrated by DAGMAR WILSON

WONDER BOOKS • NEW YORK

This book is a condensation of the famous story *Pollyanna*, especially adapted for very little children. When the children are a little older, they may want to read the original book, exactly as it was written by Eleanor H. Porter.

CONTENTS

MISS POLLY

MISS POLLY HARRINGTON entered her kitchen a little hurriedly this June morning. Nancy, washing dishes at the sink, looked up in surprise. Nancy had been working in Miss Polly's kitchen only two months, but already she knew that her mistress did not usually hurry.

"Nancy!"

"Yes, ma'am." Nancy answered cheerfully, but she still continued wiping the pitcher in her hand.

"Nancy,"—Miss Polly's voice was very stern now—"when I'm talking to you, I wish you to stop your work and listen to what I have to say."

Nancy set the pitcher down at once, with

the cloth still about it, thereby nearly tipping it over. "Yes, ma'am; I will, ma'am," she stammered, righting the pitcher and turning hastily. "I was only keepin' on with my work 'cause you specially told me this mornin' ter hurry with my dishes, ye know."

Her mistress frowned. "That will do, Nancy. I did not ask for explanations. I asked for your attention."

"Yes, ma'am." Nancy stifled a sigh. She was wondering if ever in any way she could please this woman. Nancy had known Miss Polly Harrington only as the mistress of the old Harrington homestead. That was two months before. She knew Miss Polly now as a stern, severe-faced woman who frowned if a knife clattered to the floor, or if a door banged.

"When you've finished your morning work, Nancy," Miss Polly was saying now, "you may clear the little room at the head of the stairs in the attic, and make up the cot bed. My niece, Miss Pollyanna Whittier, is coming to live with me. She is eleven years old, and will sleep in that room."

"A little girl—coming here, Miss Harrington? Oh, won't that be nice!" cried Nancy.

"Nice? Well, that isn't exactly the word I should use. However, I intend to make the best of it, of course. I am a good woman, I hope, and I know my duty."

Nancy colored hotly.

"Of course, ma'am; it was only that I thought a little girl here might—might brighten things up—for you," she faltered.

"Thank you," rejoined the lady, dryly. "I can't say, however, that I see any immediate need for that."

"But, of course, you—you'd want her, your sister's child," ventured Nancy.

Miss Polly lifted her chin haughtily.

"Well, really, Nancy, just because I happened to have a sister who was silly enough to marry and bring unnecessary children into a world that was already quite full enough, I can't see how I should particularly *want* to have the care of them myself. However, as I said before, I hope I know my duty. See that you clean the corners, Nancy."

"Yes, ma'am," sighed Nancy, picking up the half-dried pitcher.

In her own room, Miss Polly took out once more the letter which she had received two days before from the faraway Western town.

The letter was addressed to Miss Polly Harrington, Beldingsville, Vermont, and it read as follows:

DEAR MADAM: *I regret to inform you that the Rev. John Whittier died two weeks ago, leaving one child, a girl eleven years old. He left practically nothing else save a few books, for he was the pastor of this small mission church, and had a very meager salary.*

I believe he was your deceased sister's husband, but he gave me to understand the families were not on the best of terms. He thought, however, that for your sister's sake you might wish to take the child and bring her up among her own people. Hence I am writing to you.

"The little girl will be all ready to start by the time you get this letter; and if you can take her, we would appreciate it very much if you would write that she might come at once, as there is a man and his wife here who are going East very soon, and they would take her with them to Boston, and put her on the Beldingsville train.

Hoping to hear favorably from you soon, I remain,

Respectfully yours,
JEREMIAH O. WHITE.

With a frown Miss Polly folded the letter and tucked it into its envelope. She had answered it the day before, and she had said she would take the child, of course. She *hoped* she knew her duty well enough for that!— disagreeable as the task would be.

As she sat now, with the letter in her hands, her thoughts went back to her sister, Jennie, who, as a girl of twenty, had insisted upon marrying the young minister. There had been a man of wealth who had wanted her —and the family had much preferred him to the minister; but Jennie had not. She had married the minister, and had gone south with him as a home missionary's wife.

Miss Polly, looking out at the far-reaching valley below, thought of the changes twenty-five years had brought to her. She was forty now, and quite alone in the world. Father, mother, sisters—all were dead. For years, now, she had been sole mistress of the house left her by her father. People who openly pitied her lonely life had urged her to have some friend or companion to live with her; but she had not welcomed either their sympathy or their advice. She was not lonely, she said. She preferred quiet. But now—

OLD TOM AND NANCY

IN THE GARDEN that afternoon, Nancy found a few minutes in which to interview Old Tom, who had pulled weeds and shoveled the paths about the place for years.

"Mr. Tom," began Nancy, throwing a quick glance over her shoulder to make sure she was unobserved, "did you know a little girl was comin' here ter live with Miss Polly?"

"A—what?" demanded the old man, straightening his bent back with difficulty.

"A little girl—to live with Miss Polly."

"Go on with yer jokin'," scoffed unbelieving Tom. "Why don't ye tell me the sun is a-goin' ter set in the east ter-morrer?"

"But it's true. She told me so herself," maintained Nancy. "It's her niece."

The man's jaw fell.

"I wonder, now," he muttered. Then a tender light came into his faded eyes. "It must be Miss Jennie's little gal!"

"Who was Miss Jennie?"

"She was twenty when she married and went away from here long years ago. Her babies all died, I heard, except the last one; and that must be the one what's a-comin'."

"And she's goin' ter sleep in the attic—more shame ter *her!*" scolded Nancy, with another glance over her shoulder.

Old Tom frowned. The next moment a curious smile curved his lips. "I'm a-wonderin' what Miss Polly will do with a child in the house," he said.

"Humph! Well, *I*'m a-wonderin' what a child will do with Miss Polly in the house!" snapped Nancy.

The old man laughed. "I'm afraid you ain't fond of Miss Polly," he grinned.

"As if ever anybody could be fond of her!" scorned Nancy.

Old Tom smiled oddly. He stooped and began to work again. "Someone once loved her," he said slowly. "And the feller's livin' right in this town, too. But I ain't a-tellin' who. It ain't fit that I should."

THE COMING OF
POLLYANNA

IN DUE TIME came the telegram announc-
ing that Pollyanna would arrive the next
day, the twenty-fifth of June, at four o'clock.
Miss Polly read the telegram, frowned, then
climbed the stairs to the attic room.

The room contained a small bed, neatly
made, two straight-backed chairs, a wash-
stand, a bureau—without any mirror—and
a small table. There were no drapery curtains
at the dormer windows, no pictures on the
wall. All day the sun had been pouring down
upon the roof, and the little room was like
an oven. The windows had not been raised.
A big fly was buzzing at one of them now.

"Nancy," she said a few minutes later, at the kitchen door, "I found a fly upstairs in Miss Pollyanna's room. The window must have been raised at some time. I have ordered screens, but until they come I shall expect you to see that the windows remain closed. My niece will arrive tomorrow at four o'clock. I desire you to meet her at the station. Timothy will drive you over. The telegram says 'light hair, red-checked gingham dress, and straw hat.' "

Promptly at twenty minutes to four the next afternoon Timothy and Nancy drove off in the open buggy to meet the expected guest. Timothy, who was Old Tom's son, was a good-natured youth, and a good-looking one.

"I hope for her sake she's quiet and sensible, and don't drop knives nor bang doors," sighed Nancy.

"Well, if she ain't, nobody knows what'll become of the rest of us," grinned Timothy. "Imagine Miss Polly and a *noisy* kid!"

At the station, Nancy hurried to where she could best watch the passengers alight. It was not long before she saw her—a slender little girl in red-checked gingham with two braids of hair hanging down her back.

The little girl was standing quite by herself when Nancy finally did approach her.

"Are you Miss—Pollyanna?" she faltered. The next moment she found herself half smothered by two gingham-clad arms.

"Oh, I'm so glad, *glad*, GLAD to see you," cried an eager voice in her ear. "Of course I'm Pollyanna, and I'm so glad you came to meet me! I hoped you would."

"You—you did?" stammered Nancy.

"Oh, yes. I've been wondering all the way here what you looked like," cried the little girl. "And now I know, and I'm glad you look just like you do look."

Nancy was relieved just then to have Timothy come up. "This is Timothy. Maybe you have a trunk," she stammered.

"Yes, I have," nodded Pollyanna, importantly. "I've got a brand-new one. The Ladies' Aid bought it for me—and wasn't it lovely of them, when they wanted the carpet so? Of course I don't know how much red carpet a trunk could buy, but it ought to buy some, anyhow—much as half an aisle, don't you think? I've got a little thing here in my bag that Mr. Gray said was a check, and that I must give it to you before I could get my trunk. Mr. Gray is Mrs. Gray's husband. They're cousins of Deacon Carr's wife. I came East with them, and—there, here 'tis," she finished, producing the check after much fumbling in the bag she carried.

Nancy drew a long breath. Instinctively she felt that someone had to draw one—after that speech. Then she stole a glance at Timothy. Timothy's eyes were studiously turned away.

The three were off at last.

"There! Isn't this lovely? Is it far? I hope 'tis—I love to ride," sighed Pollyanna, as the wheels began to turn. "Of course, if 'tisn't far, I sha'n't mind, though, 'cause I'll be glad to get there all the sooner, you know. What a pretty street! I knew 'twas going to be pretty. Father told me—"

She stopped with a little choking breath. Nancy saw that her small chin was quivering, and that her eyes were full of tears. In a moment, however, she hurried on, with a brave lifting of her head.

"Father told me all about it. He remembered. And—and I ought to have explained before—about this red gingham dress, you know, and why I'm not in black. But there weren't any black things in the last missionary barrel—only a lady's velvet basque which Deacon Carr's wife said wasn't suitable for me at all. Of course, 'twould have been a good deal harder to be glad in black—"

"Glad!" gasped Nancy.

"Yes—that Father's gone to Heaven to be with Mother and the rest of us, you know. He said I must be glad. But it's been pretty hard to—to do it, because I—I wanted him so; and I couldn't help feeling I *ought* to have him, specially as Mother and the rest have God and all the angels, while I didn't have anybody but the Ladies' Aid. But now it'll be easier because I've got you, Aunt Polly."

Nancy's aching sympathy turned suddenly into shocked terror.

"Oh, but—but you've made an awful mistake, d-dear," she faltered. "I'm only Nancy. I ain't your Aunt Polly, at all!"

"You—you *aren't?*"

"No. I'm only Nancy, the hired girl."

"But there *is* an Aunt Polly?" demanded the child, anxiously.

"You bet your life there is," cut in Timothy.

Pollyanna relaxed visibly.

"Oh, that's all right, then. You know, she's all the aunt I've got, and I didn't know I had her for ever so long. Then Father told me. He said she lived in a lovely big house 'way on top of a hill."

"She does. You can see it now," said Nancy.

"Oh, how pretty! Is my Aunt Polly rich, Nancy?"

"Yes, Miss."

"I'm so glad. It must be perfectly lovely to have lots of money. Has she got carpets?"

"Yes, she's got carpets."

"In every room?"

"Well, in almost every room," answered Nancy, frowning suddenly at the thought of that bare little room in the attic.

THE LITTLE ATTIC ROOM

MISS POLLY HARRINGTON did not rise to meet her niece. She looked up from her book, it is true, as Nancy and the little girl appeared in the sitting-room doorway, and she held out a hand with "duty" written large on every coldly extended finger.

"How do you do, Pollyanna? I—" She had no chance to say more. Pollyanna had fairly flown across the room and flung herself into her aunt's lap.

"Oh, Aunt Polly, Aunt Polly, I don't know how to be glad enough that you let me come to live with you," she was sobbing. "You don't know how perfectly lovely it is to have you and Nancy and all this after you've had just the Ladies' Aid!"

"Very likely—though I've not had the pleasure of the Ladies' Aid's acquaintance," rejoined Miss Polly, stiffly, trying to unclasp the small, clinging fingers, and turning frowning eyes on Nancy in the doorway. "Nancy, that will do—you may go. Pollyanna, be good enough, please, to stand erect in a proper manner. I don't know yet what you look like. You had a trunk, I presume?"

"Oh, yes, indeed, Aunt Polly. I've got a beautiful trunk that the Ladies' Aid gave me. I haven't got so very much in it—of my own, I mean. The barrels haven't had many clothes for little girls in them lately; but there were all Father's books. You see, Father—"

"Pollyanna," interrupted her aunt sharply, "there is one thing that might just as well be understood at once, and that is, I do not care to have you keep talking of your father to me."

The little girl drew in her breath tremulously.

"Why, Aunt Polly, you mean—"

"We will go upstairs to your room. Your trunk is already there, I presume. I told Timothy to take it up—if you had one. You may follow me, Pollyanna."

Without speaking, Pollyanna turned and followed her aunt from the room.

"After all, I—I reckon I'm glad she doesn't want me to talk about Father," Pollyanna was thinking. "It'll be easier, maybe—if I don't talk about him. Probably, anyhow, that is why she told me not to talk about him."

She was on the stairway now. Just ahead, her aunt's black silk skirt rustled luxuriously. Behind her an open door allowed a glimpse of soft-tinted rugs and satin-covered chairs. Eagerly Pollyanna's small feet pattered behind her aunt. Still more eagerly her big blue eyes tried to look in all directions at once, that no thing in this wonderful house might be unseen. Then, abruptly, her aunt opened a door and ascended another stairway.

There was little to be seen here. A bare wall rose on either side. At the top of the stairs, wide reaches of shadowy space led to far corners where the roof came almost down to the floor, and where were stacked innumerable trunks and boxes. It was hot and stifling, too. Pollyanna saw that her aunt had thrown open a door at the right.

"There, Pollyanna, is your room, and your trunk is here, I see. Have you your key?"

Pollyanna nodded dumbly. Her eyes were a little wide and frightened.

Her aunt frowned.

"When I ask a question, Pollyanna, I prefer that you should answer aloud—not merely with your head."

"Yes, Aunt Polly."

"Thank you; that is better. I believe you have everything that you need here," she added, glancing at the well-filled towel rack and water pitcher. "I will send Nancy up to help you unpack. Supper is at six o'clock," she finished, as she left the room.

For a moment after she had gone, Pollyanna stood quite still, looking after her. Then she turned her wide eyes to the bare wall, the bare floor, the bare windows. She turned them last to the little trunk that had stood not so long before in her own little room in the faraway Western home. The next moment she stumbled blindly toward it and fell on her knees at its side, covering her face with her hands.

Nancy found her there when she came up a few minutes later.

"There, there, you poor lamb," she crooned, dropping to the floor and drawing the little girl into her arms. "Come, let's have your key and we'll get inside this trunk and take out your dresses in no time, no time."

Somewhat tearfully Pollyanna produced the key. "There aren't very many there, anyway," she faltered.

"Then they're all the sooner unpacked," declared Nancy.

Pollyanna gave a sudden radiant smile. "That's so! I can be glad of that, can't I?"

Nancy stared. "Why, of—course," she answered a little uncertainly.

At one of the windows, a few minutes later, Pollyanna clapped her hands joyously.

"Oh, Nancy, I hadn't seen this before," she breathed. "Look—'way off there, with those trees and the houses and that lovely church spire, and the river shining just like silver. Oh, I'm so glad now she let me have this room!"

Left alone, Pollyanna went back to her "picture," as she mentally designated the beautiful view from the window. It seemed as if no longer could she endure the stifling heat. The next moment the window was wide open, and Pollyanna was leaning far out, drinking in the fresh, sweet air.

She ran then to the other window. That, too, soon flew up under her eager hands. A big fly swept past her nose, and buzzed noisily about the room. Then another came, and another; but Pollyanna paid no heed. Pollyanna had made a wonderful discovery—against this window a huge tree flung great branches. To Pollyanna they looked like arms outstretched, inviting her.

Suddenly she laughed aloud.

"I believe I can do it," she chuckled. The next moment she had climbed nimbly to the window ledge. From there it was an easy matter to step to the nearest tree branch. Clinging like a monkey, she swung herself from limb to limb until the lowest branch was reached, and then landed on all fours in the soft grass.

She was at the back of the house. Before her lay a garden in which a bent old man was working. Beyond the garden a little path through an open field led up a steep hill, at the top of which a lone pine tree stood on guard beside the huge rock. To Pollyanna, at the moment, there seemed to be just one place in the world worth being in—the top of that big rock.

Fifteen minutes later the great clock in the hallway of the Harrington homestead struck six. At precisely the last stroke Nancy sounded the bell for supper.

One, two, three minutes passed. Miss Polly frowned and tapped the floor with her slipper. "Nancy," she said with decision, "my niece is late. No, you need not call her," she added severely, as Nancy made a move toward the hall door. "I told her what time supper was, and now she will have to suffer the consequences. She may as well begin at once to learn to be punctual. When she comes down, she may have bread and milk in the kitchen."

"Yes, ma'am." It was well, perhaps, that Miss Polly did not happen to be looking at Nancy's face just then.

At the earliest possible moment after supper, Nancy crept up the back stairs and thence to the attic room.

"Bread and milk, indeed!—and when the poor lamb hain't only just cried herself to sleep," she was muttering fiercely, as she softly pushed open the door. The next moment she gave a frightened cry. Then she flew downstairs and out to Old Tom in the garden.

"Mr. Tom, that blessed child's gone," she wailed, "right up into Heaven where she come from, poor lamb."

The old man straightened up.

"Gone? Heaven?" he repeated, unconsciously sweeping the brilliant sunset sky with his gaze. He stopped, stared a moment intently, then turned with a slow grin. "Well, Nancy, it do look like as if she'd tried ter get as nigh Heaven as she could, and that's a fact," he agreed, pointing with a crooked finger to where, sharply outlined against the reddening sky, a slender, wind-blown figure was poised on top of a huge rock.

THE GAME

"FOR the land's sake, Miss Pollyanna, what a scare you did give me," panted Nancy, hurrying up to the big rock. "I didn't see you go, and nobody didn't. I guess you flew right up through the roof; I do, I do."

Pollyanna skipped gleefully.

"I did, 'most—only I flew down instead of up. I came down the tree."

Nancy stopped short. "You did—what?"

"Came down the tree, outside my window."

"My stars and stockings!" gasped Nancy.

The sky was darkening fast. Pollyanna took a firmer hold of her friend's arm.

"I reckon I'm glad, after all, that you *did*

get scared—a little, 'cause then you came after me," she shivered.

"Poor little lamb! And you must be hungry, too. I—I'm afraid you'll have ter have bread and milk in the kitchen with me. Yer aunt didn't like it—because you didn't come down ter supper, ye know."

"But I couldn't. I was up here."

"Yes, but—she didn't know that, you see," observed Nancy, dryly. "I'm sorry about the bread and milk; I am, I am."

"Oh, I'm not. I like bread and milk, and I'd like to eat with you. I don't see any trouble about being glad about that."

"You don't seem ter see any trouble bein' glad about everythin'," retorted Nancy.

Pollyanna laughed softly.

"Well, that's the 'just being glad' game."

"Whatever in the world are you talkin' about?"

"Why, it's a game. Father told it to me, and it's lovely," rejoined Pollyanna.

"What is it? I ain't much on games."

"Why, we began it on some crutches that came in a missionary barrel."

"*Crutches!*"

"Yes. You see, I'd wanted a doll, and Father

had written them so; but when the barrel came, the lady wrote that there hadn't any dolls come in, but the little crutches had. So she sent 'em along as they might come in handy for some child, sometime."

"Well, I must say I can't see any game about that, about that," declared Nancy.

"Oh, yes; the game was to just find something about everything to be glad about—no matter what 'twas," rejoined Pollyanna, earnestly. "But *I* couldn't see it, either, at first," she added, with quick honesty. "Father had to tell it to me."

"Well, then, suppose *you* tell *me*," almost snapped Nancy.

"Goosey! Why, just be glad because you *don't—need—'em!*" exulted Pollyanna.

"Well, of all the queer doin's!" breathed Nancy, regarding Pollyanna with almost fearful eyes.

"Oh, but it isn't queer—it's lovely," maintained Pollyanna enthusiastically. "And we've played it ever since. And the harder 'tis, the more fun 'tis to get 'em out; only—sometimes it's almost too hard—like when your father goes to Heaven, and there isn't anybody but a Ladies' Aid left."

"Humph!" choked Nancy, trying to swallow the lump in her throat.

"Most generally it doesn't take so long," sighed Pollyanna. "I suppose, though, it'll be a little harder now, as long as I haven't anybody to play it with. Maybe Aunt Polly will play it, though," she added.

"My stars and stockings!—*her!*" breathed Nancy, behind her teeth. Then, aloud, she said doggedly: "See here, Miss Pollyanna, I ain't sayin' that I'll play it very well, and I ain't sayin' that I know how, anyway; but I'll play it with ye, after a fashion—I just will, I will!"

"Oh, Nancy!" exulted Pollyanna, giving her a rapturous hug. "That'll be splendid! Won't we have fun?"

"Er—maybe," conceded Nancy, in open doubt.

Pollyanna ate her bread and milk with good appetite. Then, at Nancy's suggestion, she went into the sitting room, where her aunt sat reading.

Miss Polly looked up coldly.

"I'm very sorry, Pollyanna, to have been obliged so soon to send you into the kitchen to eat bread and milk."

"But I was real glad you did it, Aunt Polly. I like bread and milk, and Nancy, too. You mustn't feel bad about that one bit."

Aunt Polly sat suddenly a little more erect in her chair.

"Pollyanna, it's quite time you were in bed. Nancy will give you a candle. Be careful how you handle it. Good night."

Quite as a matter of course, Pollyanna came straight to her aunt's side and gave her an affectionate hug.

"I've had such a beautiful time, so far," she sighed happily. "I know I'm going to just love living with you—but then, I knew I should before I came. Good night."

"Well, upon my soul!" ejaculated Miss Polly, half-aloud. "What a most extraordinary child!"

Fifteen minutes later, in the attic room, a lonely little girl sobbed into the tightly clutched sheet: "I know, Father-among-the-angels, I'm not playing the game one bit now —not one bit; but I don't believe even you could find anything to be glad about sleeping all alone 'way off up here in the dark—like this. If only I was near Nancy or Aunt Polly, or even a Ladies' Aider, it would be easier!"

A QUESTION OF DUTY

IT WAS nearly seven o'clock when Pollyanna awoke. The little room was cooler now, and the air blew in fresh and sweet. Outside, the birds were twittering joyously, and Pollyanna flew to the window to talk to them. She saw then that down in the garden her aunt was already out among the rosebushes.

Down the attic stairs sped Pollyanna, leaving both doors wide open. Through the hall, down the next flight, then bang through the front screened-door and around to the garden, she ran.

Aunt Polly, with the bent old man, was leaning over a rosebush when Pollyanna, gurgling with delight, flung herself upon her.

"Oh, Aunt Polly, Aunt Polly, I reckon I am glad this morning just to be alive!"

"Poll*yanna!* Is this the usual way you say good morning?"

The little girl dropped to her toes, and danced lightly up and down.

"No, only I saw you from my window, Aunt Polly, and I got to thinking how you *weren't* a Ladies' Aider, and you were my really truly aunt; and you looked so good I just had to come down and hug you!"

The bent old man turned his back suddenly. Miss Polly attempted a frown—with not her usual success—then walked away.

"Do you always work in the garden, Mr. —Man?" asked Pollyanna, interestedly.

The man turned. His lips were twitching, but his eyes looked blurred as if with tears.

"Yes, Miss. I'm Old Tom, the gardener," he answered. Timidly, he reached out a shaking hand and let it rest for a moment on her bright hair. "You are so like your mother, little Miss! I used ter know her when she was even littler than you be. You see, I used ter work in the garden—then."

"You did? Oh, please tell me about her!" exclaimed Pollyanna.

A bell sounded from the house. The next moment Nancy dashed out the back door.

"Miss Pollyanna, that bell means breakfast—mornin's," she panted, pulling the little girl to her feet and hurrying her back to the house; "and other times it means other meals. But it always means that you're ter run like time when ye hear it, no matter where ye be."

Breakfast, for the first five minutes, was a silent meal. Then Miss Polly, her disapproving eyes following the airy wings of two flies darting here and there over the table, said sternly, "Nancy, where did those flies come from?"

"I don't know, ma'am."

"I reckon maybe they're my flies, Aunt Polly," observed Pollyanna, amiably. "There were lots of them this morning having a beautiful time upstairs."

"Yours!" gasped Miss Polly. "What do you mean? Where did they come from?"

"Why, Aunt Polly, they came from out of doors, of course, through the windows. I *saw* some of them come in."

"You saw them! You mean you raised those windows without any screens?"

"Why, yes. There weren't any screens there, Aunt Polly."

"Pollyanna, I have ordered screens for those windows. I knew, of course, that it was my duty to do that. But I consider it your duty to keep your windows closed till those screens come. Flies are not only unclean and annoying, but very dangerous to health. After breakfast I will give you a little pamphlet on this matter to read."

"To read? Oh, thank you, Aunt Polly. I love to read!"

Miss Polly drew in her breath audibly, then she shut her lips together hard. She did not speak, indeed, until the meal was over. Then she rose, went to the bookcase, took out a small paper booklet, and crossed the room to her niece's side.

"This is the article I spoke of, Pollyanna. I desire you to go to your room at once and read it. I will be up in half an hour to look over your things."

Half an hour later when Miss Polly entered Pollyanna's room, she was greeted with a burst of eager enthusiasm.

"Oh, Aunt Polly, I never saw anything so perfectly lovely and interesting in my life.

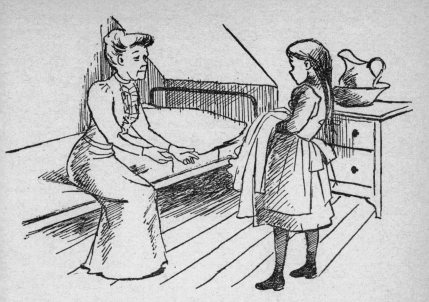

Why, I didn't suppose flies could carry such a lot of things on their feet, and—"

"That will do," observed Aunt Polly, with dignity. "Pollyanna, you may bring out your clothes now, and I will look them over. What are not suitable for you I shall give to the Sullivans, of course."

With visible reluctance Pollyanna laid down the pamphlet. She dived into her closet then, hurriedly, and brought out all the poor little dresses in both her arms.

With the tips of her fingers Miss Polly turned over the garments, so obviously made for anybody but Pollyanna. Her scrutiny finished, she turned abruptly to Pollyanna.

"You have been to school, of course, Polly-anna?"

"Oh, yes, Aunt Polly. Besides, Fath— I mean, I was taught at home some, too."

Miss Polly frowned.

"Very good. In the fall you will enter school here, of course. Meanwhile, I suppose I ought to hear you read aloud. At nine o'clock every morning you will read aloud one half-hour to me. Before that you will use the time to put this room in order. Wednesday and Saturday forenoons, after half-past nine, you will spend with Nancy in the kitchen, learning to cook. Other mornings you will sew with me. That will leave the afternoons for your music. I shall, of course, procure a teacher at once for you," she finished decisively.

Pollyanna cried out in dismay.

"Oh, but Aunt Polly, you haven't left me any time at all just to—to live."

"To live, child—what do you mean?"

"I mean *living*—doing the things you want to do: playing outdoors, reading (to myself, of course), climbing hills, talking to Mr. Tom in the garden, and Nancy, and finding out all about the houses and the people."

Miss Polly lifted her head irritably.

"Pollyanna, you *are* the most extraordinary child! You will be allowed a proper amount of playtime, of course. But, surely, it seems to me if I am willing to do my duty in seeing that you have proper care and instruction, *you* ought to be willing to do yours by seeing that that care and instruction are not ungratefully wasted."

Pollyanna looked shocked.

"Oh, Aunt Polly, as if I ever could be ungrateful—to *you!* Why, I *love you*—and you aren't even a Ladies' Aider. You're an aunt!"

"Very well; then see that you don't act ungrateful. Oh, I forgot to tell you. Timothy will drive us into town at half-past one this afternoon. Not one of your garments is fit for my niece to wear. Certainly I should be far from doing my duty by you if I should let you appear out in any one of them."

Pollyanna sighed. "Aunt Polly, please," she called wistfully, "isn't there *any* way you can be glad about all that—duty business?"

"What?" Miss Polly looked up in dazed surprise. Then, suddenly, with very red cheeks, she turned and swept angrily down the stairs. "Don't be impertinent, Pollyanna!"

POLLYANNA AND
PUNISHMENTS

FITTING Pollyanna with a new wardrobe consumed the entire afternoon. Then came supper and a delightful talk with Old Tom in the garden, and another with Nancy on the back porch, after the dishes were done.

Old Tom told Pollyanna wonderful things of her mother, that made her very happy indeed; and Nancy told her all about the little farm six miles away where lived her own mother, and her brother and sisters.

At half-past eight Pollyanna went up

to bed. The screens had not yet come, and the room was like an oven.

Just how long she lay tossing from side to side of the hot little cot, she did not know; but she finally slipped out of bed, felt her way across the room and opened her door.

Out in the main attic, all was velvet blackness save where the moon flung a path of silver halfway across the floor from the east dormer window. Pollyanna drew a quick breath and pattered straight into that silvery path, and on to the window.

She had hoped that this window might have a screen, but it did not. Outside, however, there was a wide world of fairy-like beauty, and fresh, sweet air that would feel so good to hot cheeks and hands!

As she stepped nearer and peered out, she saw something else. She saw, only a little way below the window, the wide, flat tin roof of Miss Polly's sun parlor. If only, now, her bed were out there!

Suddenly Pollyanna remembered that she had seen near this attic window a row of long white bags hanging from nails. Nancy had said that they contained winter clothing, put away for the summer. A little fearfully now,

Pollyanna felt her way to these bags, selected a nice fat soft one for a bed, and a thinner one to be doubled up for a pillow, and still another for a covering. Thus equipped, Pollyanna pattered to the moonlit window again, raised the sash, stuffed her burden through to the roof below, then let herself down after it, closing the window carefully behind her.

How deliciously cool it was! Pollyanna quite danced up and down with delight, drawing in long, full breaths of the refreshing air. Finally, with a sigh of content, she settled herself to sleep.

"I'm so glad now that the screens didn't come," she murmured, blinking up at the stars, "else I couldn't have had this!"

Downstairs in Miss Polly's room, next to the sun parlor, Miss Polly herself was hurrying into dressing gown and slippers. A minute before, she had been telephoning in a shaking voice to Timothy:

"Come up quick!—you and your father. Bring lanterns. Somebody is on the roof of the sun parlor."

Some time later, Pollyanna, just dropping off to sleep, opened her eyes to find Timothy at the top of a ladder near her, Old Tom just getting through the window, and her aunt peering out at her from behind him.

"Why, Mr. Tom—Aunt Polly!" she stammered. "Don't look so scared! It's only that I was so hot—in there. But I shut the window, Aunt Polly, so the flies couldn't carry those germ-things in."

"Pollyanna, hand those things to me at once and come in here. Of all the extraordinary children!"

To Pollyanna the air back in the attic was all the more stifling after that cool breath of the out of doors, but she did not complain. She only drew a long quivering sigh.

At the top of the stairs Miss Polly jerked out crisply, "For the rest of the night, Pollyanna, you are to sleep in my bed with me. The screens will be here tomorrow, but until then I consider it my duty to keep you where I know where you are."

Pollyanna drew in her breath.

"With you? In your bed?" she cried rapturously. "Oh, Aunt Polly, how perfectly lovely of you! My, I reckon I am glad now those screens didn't come! Wouldn't you be?"

There was no reply. Miss Polly, to tell the truth, was feeling curiously helpless.

POLLYANNA PAYS A VISIT

IT WAS not long before life at the Harrington homestead settled into something like order—though not exactly the order that Miss Polly had at first prescribed.

There were no children in the immediate neighborhood of the Harrington homestead for Pollyanna to play with. The house itself was on the outskirts of the village, and though there were other houses not far away, they did not have any boys or girls near Pollyanna's age. This, however, did not seem to disturb Pollyanna in the least.

"Oh, no, I don't mind it at all," she explained to Nancy. "I'm happy just to walk around and see the streets and the houses and watch the people. I just love people. Don't you, Nancy?"

"Well, I can't say I do—all of 'em," retorted Nancy, tersely.

Almost every pleasant afternoon found Pollyanna begging for "an errand to run," so that she might be off for a walk. And it was on these walks that frequently she met the Man.

The Man often wore a long black coat and a high silk hat—two things that the "just men" never wore. His face was clean-shaven and rather pale, and his hair, showing below his hat, was somewhat gray. He was always alone, which made Pollyanna vaguely sorry for him. One day she spoke to him.

"How do you do, sir? Isn't this a nice day?" she called cheerily, as she approached him.

The man threw a hurried glance about him, then stopped uncertainly.

"Did you speak—to me?" he asked in a sharp voice.

"Yes, sir," beamed Pollyanna. "I say, it's a nice day, isn't it?"

"Eh? Oh! Humph!" he grunted, and strode on again.

Pollyanna laughed. He was such a funny man, she thought.

The next day she saw him again.

" 'Tisn't quite so nice as yesterday, but it's pretty nice," she called out cheerfully.

"Eh? Oh! Humph!" grunted the man as before, and once again Pollyanna laughed.

When for the third time Pollyanna accosted him in much the same manner, the man stopped abruptly.

"See here, child, who are you, and why are you speaking to me every day?"

"I'm Pollyanna Whittier, and I thought you looked lonesome. I'm so glad you stopped. Now we're introduced—only I don't know your name yet."

"Well, of all the—" The man did not finish his sentence, but strode on faster than ever.

Pollyanna looked after him with a disappointed droop to her usually smiling lips.

"Maybe he didn't understand—but that was only half an introduction. I don't know *his* name, yet," she murmured.

Pollyanna was carrying calf's-foot jelly to Mrs. Snow today. Miss Polly Harrington always sent something to Mrs. Snow once a week. She said she thought that it was her duty, inasmuch as Mrs. Snow was poor, sick, and a member of her church—it was the duty of all the church members to look out for her, of course. Miss Polly did her duty by Mrs. Snow usually on Thursday afternoons—not personally, but through Nancy. Today Pollyanna had begged the privilege, and Nancy had promptly given it to her in accordance with Miss Polly's orders.

"And it's glad that I am ter get rid of it," Nancy had declared in private to Pollyanna, "though it's a shame ter be tuckin' the job off on ter you!"

"But I'd love to do it, Nancy."

"Well, you won't—after you've done it once," predicted Nancy, sourly.

"Why not?"

"Because nobody does. If folks wa'n't sorry for her, there wouldn't a soul go near her from mornin' till night, she's that cantankerous. Even the days of the week ain't run ter her mind. If it's Monday, she's bound ter say she wished 'twas Sunday. And if you take her jelly, you're pretty sure ter hear she wanted chicken. But if you *did* bring her chicken, she'd be just hankerin' for lamb broth!"

"Why, what a funny woman!" laughed Pollyanna. "She must be so surprising and— and different. I love *different* folks."

"Humph! Well, Mis' Snow's 'different,' all right—I hope, for the sake of the rest of us!" Nancy had finished grimly.

Pollyanna was thinking of these remarks today as she turned in at the gate of the shabby little cottage. A pale-faced, tired-looking young girl answered her knock at the door.

"How do you do?" began Pollyanna politely. "I'm from Miss Polly Harrington, and I'd like to see Mrs. Snow, please."

In the sickroom, after the girl had ushered her in and closed the door, Pollyanna blinked a little before she could accustom her eyes to the gloom. Then she saw, dimly outlined, a woman half-sitting up in the bed across the room. Pollyanna advanced at once.

"How do you do, Mrs. Snow? Aunt Polly says she hopes you are comfortable today, and she's sent you some calf's-foot jelly."

"Dear me! Jelly?" murmured a fretful voice. "Of course I'm very much obliged, but I was hoping 'twould be lamb broth today."

Pollyanna frowned a little.

"Why, I thought it was *chicken* you wanted when folks brought you jelly," she said.

"What?" The sick woman turned sharply.

"Why, nothing, much," apologized Polly-anna, hurriedly. "And, of course, it doesn't really make any difference. It's only that Nancy said it was chicken you wanted when we brought jelly, and lamb broth when we brought chicken—but maybe 'twas the other way, and Nancy forgot."

The sick woman pulled herself up till she sat erect in the bed—a most unusual thing for her to do, though Pollyanna did not know this.

"Well, Miss Impertinence, who are you?" she demanded.

Pollyanna laughed gleefully.

"Oh, *that* isn't my name, Mrs. Snow—and I'm so glad 'tisn't, too! I'm Pollyanna Whittier, Miss Polly Harrington's niece, and I've come to live with her. That's why I'm here this morning."

"Go to that window and pull up the curtain," the woman directed. "I should like to know what you look like!"

Pollyanna rose to her feet, but she laughed a little ruefully.

"Oh, dear! then you'll see my freckles, won't you?" she sighed, as she went to the window. "And just when I was being so glad it was dark and you couldn't see 'em. There! Now you can—oh!" She broke off excitedly, as she turned back to the bed. "I'm so glad you wanted to see me, because now I can see you! They didn't tell me you were so pretty!"

"Pretty!" scoffed the woman, bitterly.

"Why, yes. Didn't you know it?" cried Pollyanna.

"Well, no, I didn't," retorted Mrs. Snow, dryly. For fifteen years she had been too busy wishing things were different to find much time to enjoy things as they were.

"Oh, but your eyes are so big and dark, and your hair's all dark, too," cooed Pollyanna.

'But wait—just let me show you," she exclaimed, skipping over to the bureau and picking up a small hand mirror.

On the way back to the bed she stopped, eyeing the sick woman. "If you don't mind, I'd like to fix your hair just a little before I let you see it," she proposed.

"Why, I—suppose so, if you want to," permitted Mrs. Snow, grudgingly.

"Oh, thank you. I love to fix people's hair," exulted Pollyanna, carefully laying down the hand mirror and reaching for a comb.

For five minutes Pollyanna worked swiftly, deftly.

"There!" panted Pollyanna. "Now I reckon we're ready to be looked at!" And she held out the mirror in triumph.

"Humph!" grunted the sick woman, eyeing her reflection severely. "Still—'twon't last, with me tossing back and forth on the pillow as I do."

"Of course not—and I'm glad, too," nodded Pollyanna, cheerfully, "because then I can fix it again. Anyhow, I should think *you'd* be glad it's black—black shows up so much nicer on a pillow than yellow hair like mine does. I should be so glad if I only had it."

Mrs. Snow dropped the mirror and turned irritably.

"Well, you wouldn't! You wouldn't be glad for black hair nor anything else—if you had to lie here all day as I do! Just tell me something to be glad about—that's all!"

To Mrs. Snow's unbounded amazement, Pollyanna sprang to her feet and clapped her hands.

"Oh, goody! That'll be a hard one—won't it? I've got to go, now, but I'll think and think all the way home; and maybe the next time I come I can tell it to you. Good-by. I've had a lovely time!"

A little later, when Milly, Mrs. Snow's daughter, came in, the mirror still lay among the bedclothes—though it had been carefully hidden from sight.

"Why, Mother—the curtain is up!" cried Milly.

"Well, what if it is?" snapped the sick woman. "I needn't stay in the dark all my life, if I am sick, need I?"

"Why, n-no, of course not," rejoined Milly. "It's only—well, you know very well that I've tried to get you to have a lighter room for ages—and you wouldn't."

THE MAN

IT RAINED the next time Pollyanna saw the Man. She greeted him, however, with a bright smile.

"It isn't so nice today, is it?" she called blithesomely. "I'm glad it doesn't rain always, anyhow!"

The man did not even grunt this time, nor turn his head. Pollyanna decided that of course he did not hear her. The next time, therefore (which happened to be the following day), she spoke up louder.

"How do you do?" she chirped. "I'm so glad it isn't yesterday, aren't you?"

The man stopped abruptly. There was an angry scowl on his face.

"See here, little girl, we might just as well settle this thing once for all," he began testily. "I've got something besides the weather to think of. I don't know whether the sun shines or not."

Pollyanna beamed joyously.

"No, sir. I thought you didn't. That's why I told you."

"Yes, well—what?" he broke off sharply, in sudden understanding of her words.

"I say, that's why I told you—so you would notice it, you know."

"Well, of all the—" ejaculated the man. He started forward again, but after the second step he turned back, still frowning.

"See here, why don't you find someone your own age to talk to?"

"I'd like to, sir, but there aren't any 'round here, Nancy says. Still, I don't mind so very much. I like old folks just as well, maybe

better, sometimes—being used to the Ladies'
Aid, so."

"Humph! The Ladies' Aid, indeed! Is that
what you took me for?" The man's lips were
threatening to smile, but the scowl above
them was still trying to hold them grimly
stern.

The next time Pollyanna met the Man, his
eyes were gazing straight into hers, with a
quizzical directness that made his face look
really pleasant, Pollyanna thought.

"Good afternoon," he greeted her a little
stiffly. "Perhaps I'd better say right away
that I *know* the sun is shining today."

"But you don't have to tell me," nodded
Pollyanna, brightly. "I *knew* you knew it just
as soon as I saw you. I saw it in your eyes and
in your smile."

"Humph!" grunted the man.

The Man always spoke to Pollyanna after
this, and frequently he spoke first, though
usually he said little but "good afternoon."
Even that, however, was a great surprise to
Nancy, who chanced to be with Pollyanna
one day when the greeting was given.

"Sakes alive, Miss Pollyanna," she gasped,
"did that man *speak* to *you?*"

"Why, yes, he always does—now," smiled Pollyanna.

"Goodness! Do you know who—he—is?"

Pollyanna frowned and shook her head.

"He's John Pendleton. He lives all by himself in the big house on Pendleton Hill. He won't even have any one 'round ter cook for him—comes down ter the hotel for his meals three times a day. I know Sally Miner, who waits on him, and she says he hardly opens his head enough ter tell what he wants ter eat. She has ter guess it more'n half the time —only it'll be somethin' *cheap!* She knows that without no tellin'."

Pollyanna nodded sympathetically.

"I know. You have to look for cheap things when you're poor. Father and I took meals out a lot. We had beans and fish balls most generally. Does Mr. Pendleton like beans?"

"Like 'em! What if he does—or don't? Why, he's got loads of money, John Pendleton has. He could eat dollar bills, if he wanted to—and not know it."

Pollyanna giggled.

"As if anybody *could* eat dollar bills and not know it, Nancy, when they come to try to chew 'em!"

"Ho! I mean he's rich enough ter do it," shrugged Nancy. "He ain't spendin' his money, that's all. He's a-savin' of it."

"Oh, for the heathen," surmised Pollyanna. "How perfectly splendid! That's denying yourself and taking up your cross. I know. Father told me."

Nancy's lips parted, as if there were angry words all ready to come; but her eyes, resting on Pollyanna's trustful face, saw something that prevented the words being spoken.

"Humph!" she vouchsafed. Then she went on: "But, say, it *is* queer, his speakin' to you, Miss Pollyanna. He don't speak ter no one. Some says he's jest cross; and some says he's got a skeleton in his closet. And *everybody* says he's mysterious. Some years he jest travels, week in and week out."

"Oh, a missionary," nodded Pollyanna.

Nancy laughed oddly.

"Well, I didn't say that, Miss Pollyanna. When he comes back, he writes books— queer, odd books, they say. But he don't never seem ter want ter spend no money here— leastways, not for jest livin'."

"Of course not—if he's saving it for the heathen," declared Pollyanna.

A SURPRISE FOR MRS. SNOW

THE NEXT time Pollyanna went to see Mrs. Snow, she found that lady, as at first, in a darkened room.

"It's the little girl from Miss Polly's, Mother," announced Milly. Then Pollyanna found herself alone with the invalid.

"Oh, it's you, is it?" asked a fretful voice

from the bed. "I wish you had come yester-day. I *wanted* you yesterday."

"Did you? Well, I'm glad 'tisn't any farther away from yesterday than today is, then," laughed Pollyanna, advancing cheerily into the room and setting her basket down. "My! but aren't you dark here, though? I can't see you a bit," she cried, crossing to the window and pulling up the shade. "I want you to see what I've brought you."

The woman stirred restlessly.

"Just as if how it looks would make any difference in how it tastes," she scoffed—but she turned her eyes toward the basket. "Well, what is it?"

"Guess! What do you want?"

The sick woman frowned.

"Why, I don't *want* anything, as I know of," she sighed. "After all, they all taste alike!"

Pollyanna chuckled.

"This won't. Guess! If you *did* want some-thing, what would it be?"

The woman hesitated. She did not realize it herself, but she had so long been accustomed to wanting what she did not have, that to say what she *did* want seemed impossible.

"Well, of course, there's lamb broth—"

"I've got it!" crowed Pollyanna.

"But that's what I *didn't* want," sighed the sick woman, sure now of what her stomach craved. "It was chicken I wanted."

"Oh, I've got that, too," chuckled Pollyanna.

The woman turned in amazement.

"Both of them?" she demanded.

"Yes—and calf's-foot jelly," triumphed Pollyanna. "I was just bound you should have what you wanted for once; so Nancy and I fixed it. Oh, of course, there's only a little of each—but there's *some* of all of 'em! I'm so glad you did want chicken," she went on contentedly, as she lifted the three little bowls from her basket and arranged them in a row on the table. "Like enough it'll be lamb broth you want tomorrow. There! Oh, I 'most forgot, but I've thought it up, Mrs. Snow—what you can be glad about."

"*Glad* about! What do you mean?"

"Why, don't you remember? You asked me to tell you something to be glad about. I found it, too. But '*twas* hard. It's all the more fun, though, when 'tis hard. I couldn't think of anything for a while. Then I got it."

"Did you, really? Well, what is it?" Mrs. Snow's voice was sarcastically polite.

Pollyanna drew a long breath.

"I thought—how glad you could be—that other folks weren't like you—all sick in bed like this, you know," she announced.

Mrs. Snow stared. Her eyes were angry.

"And now I'll tell you the game," proposed Pollyanna. "It'll be just lovely for you to play. You see, it's like this." And she began to tell of the doll that did not come.

The story was just finished when Milly appeared at the door.

"Your aunt is wanting you, Miss Pollyanna," she said with dreary listlessness. "She telephoned down to the Harlows' across the way. She says you're to hurry—that you've got some practicing to make up before dark."

Pollyanna rose reluctantly.

"All right," she sighed. "I'll hurry." Suddenly she laughed. "I suppose I ought to be glad I've got legs to hurry with, hadn't I, Mrs. Snow?"

There was no answer. Mrs. Snow's eyes were closed. But Milly, whose eyes were wide open with surprise, saw that there were tears on the wasted cheeks.

One by one the July days passed. To Pollyanna, they were happy days, indeed. She often told her aunt, joyously, how very happy they were. Whereupon her aunt would usually reply, wearily:

"Very well, Pollyanna. I am gratified, of course, that they are happy, but I trust that they are profitable, as well."

"Do you mean that it wouldn't be enough then, Aunt Polly, that they should be just happy days?" she asked wistfully.

"That is what I mean, Pollyanna."

"They must be pro-fi-ta-ble as well?"

"Certainly."

"What is being pro-fi-ta-ble?"

"Why, it—it's just being profitable—having profit, something to show for it, Pollyanna. What an extraordinary child you are!"

"Then just being glad isn't pro-fi-ta-ble?" Pollyanna asked.

"Certainly not."

"Oh, dear! Then you wouldn't like it, of course. I'm afraid, now, you won't ever play the game, Aunt Polly."

"Game? What game?"

"Why, that Father—" Pollyanna clapped her hands to her lips. "N-nothing," she said.

It was that afternoon that Pollyanna, coming down from her attic room, met her aunt on the stairway.

"Why, Aunt Polly, how perfectly lovely!" she cried. "You were coming up to see me! Come right in. I love company," she finished, scampering up the stairs and throwing her door wide open.

Now Miss Polly had not been intending to call on her niece. She had been planning to look for a certain white wool shawl in the cedar chest near the east window. But to her unbounded surprise now, she found herself, not in the main attic before the cedar chest, but in Pollyanna's little room sitting in one of the straight-backed chairs. So many, many times since Pollyanna came, Miss Polly had found herself like this, doing some utterly unexpected, surprising thing, quite unlike the thing she had set out to do!

"I love company," said Pollyanna, again, flitting about as if she were dispensing the hospitality of a palace; " 'specially since I've had this room, all mine, you know. *Now* I just love it, even if it hasn't got the carpets and curtains and pictures that I'd been want—" With a painful blush Pollyanna stopped short.

"What's that, Pollyanna?"

"N-nothing. I didn't mean to say it."

"Probably not," returned Miss Polly, coldly, "but you did say it, so suppose we have the rest of it."

"But it wasn't anything, only that I'd been kind of planning on pretty carpets and lace curtains and things, you know. But, of course—"

"*Planning* on them!" interrupted Miss Polly, sharply.

Pollyanna blushed still more painfully.

"I ought not to have, of course, Aunt Polly," she apologized. "It was only because I'd always wanted them and hadn't had them, I suppose. But, truly, Aunt Polly, it wasn't but just a minute—I mean, a few minutes— before I was being glad that the bureau *didn't* have a looking-glass, because it didn't show my freckles; and there couldn't be a nicer picture than the one out my window there; and you've been so good to me, that—"

Miss Polly rose suddenly to her feet. Her face was very red.

"That will do, Pollyanna," she said stiffly. "You have said quite enough, I'm sure."

Less than twenty-four hours later, Miss Polly said to Nancy, crisply:

"Nancy, you may move Miss Pollyanna's things downstairs to the room directly beneath. I have decided to have my niece sleep there for the present."

"Yes, ma'am," said Nancy aloud.

"Oh, glory!" said Nancy to herself.

INTRODUCING JIMMY

AUGUST came. August brought several surprises and some changes.

First there was the kitten.

Pollyanna found the kitten mewing pitifully some distance down the road. When questioning failed to find anyone who claimed it, Pollyanna brought it home at once, as a matter of course.

"And I was glad I didn't find anyone who owned it, too," she told her aunt in happy confidence, " 'cause I wanted to bring it home all the time. I love kitties. I told everybody we should keep it, if I didn't find where it belonged."

Miss Polly opened her lips and tried to speak, but in vain. The curious helpless feeling that had been hers so often since Pollyanna's arrival, had her now fast in its grip.

"Of course I knew," hurried on Pollyanna, gratefully, "that you wouldn't let a dear little lonesome kitty go hunting for a home when you'd just taken *me* in. Why, *I* had the Ladies' Aid, you know, and kitty didn't have anybody."

"But, Pollyanna," remonstrated Miss Polly, "I don't—" But Pollyanna was already halfway to the kitchen, calling:

"Nancy, Nancy, just see this dear little kitty that Aunt Polly is going to bring up along with me!"

The next day it was a dog. And again Miss Polly found herself figuring as a kind protector and an angel of mercy.

When, in less than a week, however, Pollyanna brought home a small, ragged boy, and confidently claimed the same protection for him, Miss Polly did have something to say. It happened after this wise.

On a pleasant Thursday morning Pollyanna saw the boy sitting by the roadside, whittling half-heartedly at a small stick.

"Hullo," smiled Pollyanna, engagingly.

The boy stirred restlessly, gave her a surprised look, and began to whittle again at his stick, with the dull, broken-bladed knife in his hand.

Pollyanna hesitated, then dropped herself comfortably down on the grass near him. She had sighed at times for some companion of her own age.

"My name's Pollyanna Whittier," she began pleasantly. "What's yours?"

Again the boy stirred restlessly. He even almost got to his feet. But he settled back.

"Jimmy Bean," he grunted.

"Good! Now we're introduced. I'm glad you did your part—some folks don't, you know. I live at Miss Polly Harrington's house. Where do you live?"

"Nowhere."

"Nowhere! Why, you can't do that—everybody lives somewhere," asserted Pollyanna.

"Well, I don't—just now. I'm huntin' up
a new place."

"Oh! Where is it?"

The boy regarded her with scornful eyes.

"Silly! As if I'd be a-huntin' for it—if I
knew!"

Pollyanna tossed her head a little. This was
not a nice boy, and she did not like to be
called "silly." Still, he was somebody besides
—old folks.

"Where did you live—before?" she que-
ried.

"Well, if you ain't the beat'em for askin'
questions!" sighed the boy impatiently.

"I have to be," retorted Pollyanna calmly,

"else I couldn't find out a thing about you. If you'd talk more, I wouldn't talk so much."

The boy gave a short laugh. It was a sheepish laugh, and not quite a willing one, but his face looked a little pleasanter when he spoke this time.

"All right then—here goes! I'm Jimmy Bean, and I'm ten years old goin' on eleven. I come last year ter live at the Orphans' Home, but they've got so many kids, there ain't much room for me, an' I wa'n't never wanted, anyhow, I don't believe. So I've quit. I'm goin' ter live somewheres else—but I hain't found the place, yet. I'd *like* a home— one, ye know, with a mother in it, instead of a matron. If ye has a home, ye has folks; an' I hain't had folks since—Dad died. I've tried four houses, but—they didn't want me— though I said I expected ter work, 'course. There! Is that all you want ter know?" The boy's voice had broken a little over the last two sentences.

"Why, what a shame!" sympathized Pollyanna. "Aunt Polly'll take you—I know she will! Didn't she take me? And didn't she take Fluffy and Buffy, when they didn't have any one to love them, or any place to go? And they're only cats and dogs. Oh, come, I know Aunt Polly'll take you! You don't know how good and kind she is!"

Jimmy Bean's thin little face brightened.

"Honest Injun? Would she, now? I'd work, ye know, an' I'm real strong!"

"Of course she would! There's rooms—heaps of 'em," she continued, springing to her feet, and tugging at his arm. "It's an awful big house. Maybe, though," she added a little anxiously, "you'll have to sleep in the attic room. I did, at first. But there's screens there now, so 'twon't be so hot, and the flies can't get in, either, to bring in the germ-things on their feet."

When the house was reached, Pollyanna piloted her companion straight into the presence of her amazed aunt.

"Oh, Aunt Polly," she triumphed. "Just look a-here! I've got something ever so much nicer, even, than Fluffy and Buffy for you to bring up. It's a real live boy. He won't mind a bit sleeping in the attic, at first, you know, and he says he'll work."

Miss Polly grew white, then very red. She did not quite understand, but she thought she understood enough.

"Pollyanna, what does this mean? Who is this dirty little boy? Where did you find him?"

The "dirty little boy" fell back a step and looked toward the door. Pollyanna laughed.

"There, if I didn't forget to tell you his name! This is Jimmy Bean, Aunt Polly."

"Well, what is he doing here?"

"Why, Aunt Polly, I just told you!" Pollyanna's eyes were wide with surprise. "He's for you. I brought him home—so he could live here, you know."

Miss Polly dropped back in her chair and raised a shaking hand to her throat. With a visible struggle, however, she pulled herself suddenly erect.

"That will do, Pollyanna. This is the most

absurd thing you've done yet. As if tramp cats and mangy dogs weren't bad enough, you must bring home ragged little beggars from the street, who—"

There was a sudden stir from the boy. His eyes flashed and his chin came up.

"I ain't a beggar, marm, an' I don't want nothin' o' you. I wouldn't have come ter your old house, anyhow, if this 'ere girl hadn't 'a' made me, a-tellin' me how you was so good an' kind that you'd be jest dyin' ter take me in. So, there!" And he wheeled about and stalked from the room.

"Oh, Aunt Polly," choked Pollyanna, "I thought you'd be *glad* to have him here!"

Miss Polly raised her hand with a peremptory gesture of silence. "Pollyanna," she cried sharply, "*will* you stop using that word! It's 'glad'—'glad'—'glad,' from morning till night, until I think I shall grow wild!"

From sheer amazement Pollyanna's jaw dropped.

"Why, Aunt Polly," she breathed, "I should think you'd be glad to have me gl—. Oh!" she broke off, clapping her hand to her lips.

Before the boy had reached the end of the driveway, Pollyanna overtook him.

"Boy! Boy! Jimmy Bean, I want you to know how—how sorry I am," she panted.

"Sorry nothin'. I ain't blamin' you," retorted the boy. "But I ain't no beggar!" he added, with sudden spirit.

"Of course you aren't! But you mustn't blame auntie," appealed Pollyanna. "Probably I didn't do the introducing right, anyhow. I'll tell you what I *will* do! The Ladies' Aid meets this afternoon. I heard Aunt Polly say so. I'll lay your case before them. That's what Father always did, when he wanted anything—educating the heathen and new carpets, you know."

The boy turned fiercely.

"Well, I ain't a heathen or a new carpet. Besides—what is a Ladies' Aid?"

"It's—it's—why, it's just a lot of ladies that meet and sew and give suppers and raise money and—and talk. There'd be some of 'em, I know, that would be glad to give you a home. I'll let you know tomorrow."

"Where?"

"By the road, where I found you today."

"All right. I'll be there." The boy paused before he went on slowly: "Maybe I'd better go back, then, for ter-night, ter the Home."

BEFORE THE LADIES' AID

D INNER, which came at noon in the Harrington homestead, was a silent meal on the day of the Ladies' Aid meeting. Pollyanna, it is true, tried to talk; but she did not make a success of it, chiefly because four times she was obliged to break off a "glad" in the middle of it. The fifth time it happened, Miss Polly moved her head wearily.

"There, there, child, say it, if you want to," she sighed. "I'm sure I'd rather you did than not, if it's going to make all this fuss."

Pollyanna's puckered little face cleared.

"Oh, thank you. I'm afraid it would be pretty hard not to say it. You see I've played it so long."

"You've—what?" demanded Aunt Polly.

"Played it—the game, you know, that Father—" Pollyanna stopped with a painful blush at finding herself so soon again on forbidden ground.

Aunt Polly frowned and said nothing. The rest of the meal was a silent one.

Pollyanna was not sorry to hear Aunt Polly tell the minister's wife over the telephone, a little later, that she would not be at the Ladies' Aid meeting that afternoon, owing to a headache. She could not forget that Aunt Polly had called Jimmy Bean a little beggar; and she did not want Aunt Polly to call him that—before the Ladies' Aid.

Quietly, but with confident courage, Pollyanna ascended the chapel steps later that afternoon, pushed open the door and entered the vestibule. A soft babel of feminine chatter and laughter came from the main room. Hesitating only a brief moment, Pollyanna pushed open one of the inner doors.

The chatter dropped to a surprised hush. Pollyanna advanced a little timidly.

"How do you do, Ladies' Aiders?" she faltered politely. "I'm Pollyanna Whittier. I— I reckon some of you know me, maybe."

The silence could almost be felt now. Some

of the ladies did know this rather extraordinary niece of their fellow-member, and nearly all had heard of her.

"I—I've come to—to lay the case before you," stammered Pollyanna, after a moment.

There was a slight rustle.

"Yes, dear. What is it?"

"Well, it—it's Jimmy Bean," sighed Pollyanna. "He hasn't any home except the Orphan one, and they're full, and don't want him, anyhow, he thinks, so he wants another. He wants one of the common kind, that has a mother instead of a matron in it. He's ten years old, going on eleven. I thought some of you might like him—to live with you, you know. Oh, I forgot to say—he will work."

Still there was silence. Then, coldly, one or two women began to question her. After a time, they all had the story and began to talk among themselves.

Pollyanna listened with growing anxiety. Some of what was said she could not understand. She did gather, however, that there was no woman there who had a home to give him, though every woman seemed to think that some of the others might take him, as there were several who had no little boys of their own already in their homes. Then she heard the minister's wife suggest timidly that they might perhaps assume his support and education instead of sending quite so much money this year to the little boys in India.

A great many ladies talked then, and several of them talked all at once. It seemed that their society was famous for its offering to Hindu missions, and several said they should die of mortification if it should be less this year. Some of what was said sounded almost as if they did not care at all what the money *did*, so long as the sum opposite the name of their society in a certain "report" headed the list. It was all very confusing, and not quite pleasant, so that Pollyanna was glad, indeed, when at last she found herself outside in the hushed, sweet air—only she was very sorry, too: for she knew it was not going to be easy, or anything but sad, to tell Jimmy Bean tomorrow that the Ladies' Aid had decided that they would rather send all their money to bring up the little India boys than to save out enough to bring up one little boy in their own town, for which they would not get "a bit of credit in the report," according to the tall lady who wore spectacles.

IN PENDLETON WOODS

POLLYANNA had not turned her steps toward home, when she left the chapel, for she was sure that nothing would do her quite so much good as a walk through the green quiet of Pendleton Woods. Up Pendleton Hill, therefore, she climbed steadily.

Suddenly Pollyanna lifted her head and listened. A dog had barked some distance ahead. A moment later he came dashing toward her, still barking.

"Hullo, doggie!" Pollyanna snapped her fingers at the dog and looked expectantly down the path. She had seen the dog once before, she was sure. He had been then with the Man, Mr. John Pendleton.

The dog, as even Pollyanna could see, was

acting strangely, giving little short, sharp yelps, as if of alarm. Every quiver of his little brown body, and every glance from his beseeching brown eyes was so eloquent that at last Pollyanna understood, turned, and followed him.

Straight ahead, now, the little dog dashed madly; and it was not long before Pollyanna came upon the reason for it all: a man lying motionless at the foot of a steep, overhanging mass of rock a few yards from the side path.

A twig cracked sharply under Pollyanna's foot, and the man turned his head. With a cry of dismay Pollyanna ran to his side.

"Mr. Pendleton! Oh, are you hurt?"

"Hurt? Oh, no! I'm just taking a siesta in the sunshine," snapped the man irritably. "See here, how much do you know? What can you do? Have you got any sense?"

"Why, Mr. Pendleton, I—I don't know so very much, and I can't do a great many things; but most of the Ladies' Aiders, except Mrs. Rawson, said I had real good sense. I heard 'em say so one day."

The man smiled grimly.

"There, there, child, I beg your pardon, I'm sure. It's only this confounded leg of mine. Now listen." He paused, and with some difficulty reached his hand into his trousers pocket and brought out a bunch of keys, singling out one between his thumb and forefinger. "Straight through the path there, about five minutes' walk, is my house. This key will admit you to the side door. Go straight through the vestibule and hall to the door at the end. On the big, flat-topped desk in the middle of the room is a telephone. Hunt up Dr. Thomas Chilton's number, call him, and tell him that John Pendleton is at the foot of Little Eagle Ledge with a broken leg, and to come at once."

"A broken leg? Oh, Mr. Pendleton, how perfectly awful!" shuddered Pollyanna. "But I'm so glad I came! Can't *I* do—"

"Yes, you can—but evidently you won't! *Will* you go and do what I ask and stop talking," moaned the man, faintly. And, with a little sobbing cry, Pollyanna went.

It was not long before she came in sight of the house. Pausing only a moment, she sped across the big neglected lawn and around the house to the side door. Her fingers were anything but skillful in their efforts to turn the bolt in the lock, but at last the heavy, carved door swung slowly back on its hinges.

Looking neither to the right nor the left, Pollyanna fairly ran through the hall to the door at the end and opened it.

In due time she had Dr. Chilton on the telephone, and was tremblingly delivering her message. This done, she hung up the receiver and drew a long breath of relief.

Only a brief glance did Pollyanna give about her. Then, with a confused vision in her eyes of crimson draperies, book-lined walls, a littered floor, an untidy desk, and everywhere dust, dust, dust, she fled back through the hall.

In what seemed an incredibly short time, Pollyanna was back at the man's side.

"The doctor will be right up just as soon as possible," Pollyanna told him. "He said he knew just where you were, so I didn't stay to show him. I wanted to be with you."

"Did you?" smiled the man, grimly. "I should think you might find pleasanter companions."

"Do you mean—because you're so—cross?"

"Thanks for your frankness. Yes."

Pollyanna laughed softly.

"But you're only cross *outside*—you aren't cross inside a bit!"

"Indeed! How do you know that?"

"Oh, lots of ways; there—like that—the way you act with the dog," she added, pointing to the long, slender hand that rested on the dog's sleek head near him. "It's funny how dogs and cats know the insides of folks better than other folks do, isn't it? Say, I'm going to hold your head," she finished.

Minute by minute the time passed. The sun dropped lower in the west and the shadows grew deeper under the trees. Pollyanna sat so still she hardly seemed to breathe.

At last the dog pricked up his ears and whined softly. The next moment three men appeared, carrying a stretcher and various other articles.

The tallest of the party—a smooth-shaven, kind-eyed man whom Pollyanna knew by sight as "Dr. Chilton"—advanced cheerily.

"Well, my little lady, playing nurse?"

"Oh, no, sir," smiled Pollyanna. "I've only held his head—I haven't given him medicine. But I'm glad I was here."

"So am I," nodded the doctor, as he turned his attention to the injured man.

JUST A MATTER OF JELLY

A T THE appointed place the next afternoon, Pollyanna met Jimmy Bean according to agreement. Jimmy showed keen disappointment that the Ladies' Aid preferred a little India boy to himself.

"Well, maybe 'tis natural," he sighed. "Of course, things you don't know about are always nicer'n things you do, same as the pertater on t'other side of the plate is always the biggest. But I wish I looked that way ter somebody 'way off. Wouldn't it be jest great, now, if only somebody over in India wanted *me?*"

Pollyanna clapped her hands.

"Why, of course! That's the very thing, Jimmy! I'll write to *my* Ladies' Aiders about you. They aren't over in India. They're only out West—but that's awful far away, just the same. You wait. I'll write 'em."

"All right—but don't furgit ter say I'll work fur my board an' keep," put in Jimmy. "I ain't no beggar, an' biz'ness is biz'ness, even with Ladies' Aiders, I'm thinkin'." He hesitated, then added: "An' I s'pose I better stay where I be fur a spell yet—till you hear."

"Of course," nodded Pollyanna emphatically. "Then I'll know just where to find you. And they'll take you—I'm sure you're far enough away for that."

It was about a week after the accident in Pendleton Woods that Pollyanna said to her aunt one morning:

"Aunt Polly, please, would you mind very much if I took Mrs. Snow's calf's-foot jelly this week to someone else? I'm sure Mrs. Snow wouldn't mind—this once."

"Dear me, Pollyanna, what *are* you up to now?" sighed her aunt.

"Nothing, Aunt Polly, truly, that you would mind, I'm sure. You let me take jelly to *her*, so I thought you would to *him*—this once."

" 'Him'?"

"The Man. I mean, Mr. John Pendleton."

Miss Polly almost sprang from her chair.

"John Pendleton!"

"Yes. Nancy told me his name. Maybe you know him."

Miss Polly did not answer this. Instead she asked, "Do *you* know him?"

Pollyanna nodded.

"Oh, yes. He always speaks and smiles— now. He's only cross *outside*, you know. I'll go and get the jelly. Nancy had it 'most fixed when I came in," finished Pollyanna, already halfway across the room.

"Pollyanna, wait!" Miss Polly's voice was suddenly very stern. "I would prefer that Mrs. Snow had that jelly today—as usual."

Pollyanna's face fell.

"Oh, but Aunt Polly, *hers* will last. She can always be sick and have things, you know; but *his* is just a broken leg, and legs don't last—I mean, broken ones. He's had it a whole week now."

"Yes, I remember. I heard Mr. John Pendleton had met with an accident," said Miss Polly, a little stiffly. "But I do not care to be sending jelly to John Pendleton."

"I know, he is cross—outside," admitted Pollyanna, sadly, "so I suppose you don't like him. But I wouldn't say 'twas you sent it. I'd say 'twas me. I'd be glad to send him jelly."

Miss Polly began to shake her head again. Then, suddenly, she stopped, and asked in a curiously quiet voice:

"Does he know who you—are, Pollyanna?"

The little girl sighed.

"I reckon not. I told him my name, once, but he never calls me it—never."

"Does he know where you live?"

"Oh, no. I never told him that."

"Then he doesn't know you're my—niece?"

"I don't think so."

For a moment there was silence. Then Miss Polly roused herself with a start.

"Very well, Pollyanna," she said at last, "you may take the jelly to Mr. Pendleton as your own gift. But understand: I do not send it. Be very sure that he does not think I do!"

"Yes'm—no'm—thank you, Aunt Polly," exulted Pollyanna.

DR. CHILTON

A FAMILIAR-looking small dog bounded up the steps to greet Pollyanna when she made her second visit to the house of Mr. John Pendleton, but there was a slight delay before a woman opened the door.

"If you please, I've brought some calf's-foot jelly for Mr. Pendleton," smiled Pollyanna.

"Thank you," said the woman, reaching for the bowl in the little girl's hand. "Who shall I say sent it? And it's calf's-foot jelly?"

The doctor, coming into the hall at that moment, heard the woman's words and saw the disappointed look on Pollyanna's face.

"Ah! Some calf's-foot jelly?" he asked genially. "That will be fine! Maybe you'd like to see our patient, eh?"

"Oh, yes, sir," beamed Pollyanna. And the woman, in obedience to a nod from the doctor, led the way down the hall at once.

Behind the doctor, a young man gave a disturbed exclamation.

"But, Doctor, didn't Mr. Pendleton give orders not to admit anyone?"

"Oh, yes," nodded the doctor, imperturbably. "But I'm giving orders now. You don't know, of course, but that little girl is better than a bottle of tonic any day. If anything or anybody can take the grouch out of Pendleton this afternoon, she can. I wish I could prescribe her as I would a box of pills."

Pollyanna, meanwhile, was being escorted through the great library at the end of the hall, and saw at once that great changes had taken place. The book-lined walls and the crimson curtains were the same, but there was no litter, no untidiness on the desk, and not so much as a grain of dust in sight.

The next moment Pollyanna found herself alone with a very cross-looking man lying flat on his back in bed.

"See here, didn't I say—" began an angry voice. "Oh, it's you!" it broke off not very graciously, as Pollyanna advanced.

"Yes, sir," smiled Pollyanna. "Oh, I'm so glad they let me in! You see, at first the lady 'most took my jelly, and I was so afraid I wasn't going to see you at all. Then the doctor came, and he said I might. Wasn't he lovely to let me see you?"

In spite of himself, the man's lips twitched into a smile; but all he said was "Humph!"

"And I've brought you some calf's-foot jelly," resumed Pollyanna. "I hope you like it."

"Never ate it." The fleeting smile had gone, and the scowl had come back.

For a brief instant Pollyanna's countenance showed disappointment, but it cleared as she set the bowl of jelly down.

"Didn't you? Well, if you didn't, then you can't know you *don't* like it, anyhow, can you? So I reckon I'm glad you haven't, after all. Now, if you knew—"

"Yes, yes; well, there's one thing I know

all right, and that is that I'm flat on my back right here this minute, and that I'm liable to stay here—till doomsday, I guess."

. Pollyanna looked shocked.

"Oh, no! It couldn't be till doomsday, you know, when the angel Gabriel blows his trumpet, unless it should come quicker than we think it will. What I mean is, that legs don't last—broken ones, you know—like lifelong invalids, same as Mrs. Snow has got. So yours won't last till doomsday at all. I should think you could be glad of that."

"Oh, I am," retorted the man grimly.

"And you didn't break but one. You can be

glad 'twasn't two." Pollyanna was warming to her task.

"Of course! So fortunate," sniffed the man, with uplifted eyebrows. "Looking at it from that standpoint, I suppose I might be glad I wasn't a centipede and didn't break fifty!"

Pollyanna chuckled.

"Oh, that's the best yet," she crowed. "And you can be glad—"

"Oh, of course," interrupted the man, sharply, all the old bitterness coming back to his voice. "I can be glad, too, for all the rest, I suppose—the nurse, and the doctor, and that confounded woman in the kitchen!"

"Why, yes, sir—only think how bad 'twould be if you *didn't* have them!"

"As if that wasn't the very thing that was at the bottom of the whole matter," retorted the man, testily. "And yet you expect me to say I'm glad because of a fool woman who disarranges the whole house and calls it 'regulating,' and a man who aids and abets her in it, and calls it 'nursing,' to say nothing of the doctor who eggs 'em both on—and the whole bunch, meanwhile, expecting me to pay them for it, and pay them well, too!"

Pollyanna frowned sympathetically.

"Yes, I know. *That* part is too bad—about the money—when you've been denying yourself, and saving it for the heathen. You see, I found out about it. Why, Mr. Pendleton, that's one of the ways I knew you weren't cross inside. Nancy told me."

The man's jaw dropped.

"Nancy told you I was saving money for the—! Well, may I inquire who Nancy is?"

"Our Nancy. She works for Aunt Polly—Miss Polly Harrington. I live with her."

The man made a sudden movement.

"Miss—Polly—Harrington!" he breathed. "You live with—*her?*"

"Yes. I'm her niece. She's taken me to bring up—on account of my mother, you know," faltered Pollyanna, in a low voice. "She was her sister. And after Father—went to be with her, there wasn't anyone left for me but the Ladies' Aid, so she took me."

The man did not answer. His face, as he lay back on the pillow now, was very white—so white that Pollyanna was frightened.

"I reckon maybe I'd better go now," she proposed. "I—I hope you'll like—the jelly."

The man turned his head suddenly, and opened his eyes. There was a curious longing in their dark depths which even Pollyanna saw, and at which she marvelled.

"And so you are—Miss Polly Harrington's niece," he said gently.

"Yes, sir."

"But—you don't mean—you can't mean that it was Miss Polly Harrington who sent that jelly—to me?" he said slowly.

Pollyanna looked distressed.

"N-no, sir, she didn't. She said I must be very sure not to let you think she did send it. But I—"

"I thought as much," vouchsafed the man, turning away his head. And Pollyanna, still more distressed, tiptoed from the room.

"Well, Miss Pollyanna, may I have the pleasure of seeing you home?" asked the doctor smilingly. "I started to drive on a few minutes ago. Then it occurred to me that I'd wait for you."

"Thank you, sir. I'm glad you did. I just love to ride," beamed Pollyanna.

"Do you?" smiled the doctor. "Well, as near as I can judge, there are a good many things you 'love' to do—eh?" he added, as they drove briskly away.

Pollyanna laughed.

"Why, I don't know. I reckon perhaps there are," she admitted. "I like to do 'most everything that's *living*. Of course I don't like the other things very well—sewing, and reading out loud, and all that. But *they* aren't *living*."

"No? What are they, then?"

"Aunt Polly says they're 'learning to live,' " sighed Pollyanna, with a rueful smile. "But I don't see it that way at all. I don't think you have to *learn* how to live."

The doctor drew a long sigh.

"I'm afraid some of us—do have to, little girl," he said. Then, for a time he was silent. Pollyanna, stealing a glance at his face, felt vaguely sorry for him. He looked so sad. She wished, uneasily, that she could "do something." It was this, perhaps, that caused her to say in a timid voice:

"Dr. Chilton, I should think being a doctor would be the very gladdest kind of a business there was."

" 'Gladdest!' When I see so much suffering always, everywhere I go?" he cried.

She nodded.

"I know; but you're *helping* it—don't you see? And of course you're glad to help it! And so that makes you the gladdest of any of us, all the time."

The doctor's eyes filled with sudden hot tears. The doctor's life was a lonely one. He had no wife and no home save his two-room office in a boarding house. His profession was very dear to him. Looking now into Pollyanna's shining eyes, he felt as if a loving hand had been suddenly laid on his head in blessing.

"God bless you, little girl," he said unsteadily. Then, with the bright smile his patients knew and loved so well, he added: "And I'm thinking, after all, that it was the doctor, as much as his patients, that needed that tonic!"

The doctor left Pollyanna at the door and then drove away. A moment later, Pollyanna found her aunt in the sitting room.

"Who was that man—the one who drove into the yard, Pollyanna?" questioned the lady a little sharply.

"Why, Aunt Polly, that was Dr. Chilton! Don't you know him?"

"Dr. Chilton! What was he doing—here?"

"He drove me home. Oh, and I gave the jelly to Mr. Pendleton, and—"

Miss Polly lifted her head quickly.

"Pollyanna, he did not think I sent it?"

"Oh, no, Aunt Polly. I told him you didn't."

Miss Polly grew a sudden vivid pink.

"You *told* him I didn't!"

Pollyanna opened her eyes wide at the dismay in her aunt's voice.

"Why, Aunt Polly, you *said* to!"

Aunt Polly sighed.

"I *said*, Pollyanna, that I did not send it, and for you to be very sure that he did not think I *did*—which is a very different matter from *telling* him outright that I did not send it." And she turned vexedly away.

"Dear me! Well, I don't see where the difference is," sighed Pollyanna.

A RED ROSE AND
A LACE SHAWL

IT WAS ON a rainy day about a week after
Pollyanna's visit to Mr. John Pendleton
that Miss Polly, to her helpless amazement,
found herself in a low chair before the dressing table, her hair tumbling about her ears
under ten eager, but very gentle fingers.

"Oh, my, what pretty hair you've got,"
prattled Pollyanna. "And there's so much
more of it than Mrs. Snow has, too! But, of
course, you need more, anyhow, because
you're well and can go to places where folks
can see it. My, I reckon folks'll be glad when
they do see it—and surprised, too, 'cause
you've hidden it for so long!"

"Pollyanna!" gasped a stifled but shocked voice from a veil of hair. "I—I'm sure I don't know why I'm letting you do this silly thing."

"Oh, I just love to do folks' hair," purred Pollyanna, contentedly. "I did quite a lot of the Ladies' Aiders'. Oh, Aunt Polly, I've just happened to think of something!"

Before she could move, then, Miss Polly felt a folded something slipped across her eyes and tied in the back.

"Pollyanna, Pollyanna! What are you doing?" she cried.

Pollyanna chuckled.

"That's just what I don't want you to know, Aunt Polly, so I tied on the handkerchief. Now sit still. It won't take but just a minute."

"But, Pollyanna," began Miss Polly, struggling blindly to her feet, "you must take this off! You—child, child! What *are* you doing?" she gasped.

Pollyanna only chuckled the more gleefully. With trembling fingers she was draping about her aunt's shoulders the fleecy folds of a beautiful lace shawl.

Her task completed, Pollyanna pulled her aunt toward the sun parlor where she could see a red rose blooming on the trellis.

"Where are you taking me?" recoiled Aunt Polly, trying to hold herself back.

"It's just to the sun parlor—only a minute!" panted Pollyanna, reaching for the rose and thrusting it into the soft hair above Miss Polly's left ear. "There!" she exulted, untying the knot of the handkerchief.

For one dazed moment Miss Polly looked at her bedecked self, and at her surroundings; then she gave a low cry and fled to her room. Pollyanna, following the direction of her aunt's last dismayed gaze, saw, through the open windows of the sun parlor, the horse and gig turning into the driveway. She recognized at once the man who held the reins.

Delightedly she leaned forward.

"Dr. Chilton, Dr. Chilton! Did you want to see me? I'm up here."

"Yes," smiled the doctor, a little gravely. "Will you come down, please?"

In the bedroom Pollyanna found a flushed-faced, angry-eyed woman plucking at the pins that held a lace shawl in place.

"Pollyanna, how could you?" moaned the woman. "To think of your rigging me up like this, and then letting me—*be seen!*"

Pollyanna stopped in dismay.

"But you looked lovely—perfectly lovely, Aunt Polly. And—"

"'Lovely!'" scorned the woman, flinging the shawl to one side and attacking her hair with shaking fingers.

"Oh, dear! And you did look so pretty," almost sobbed Pollyanna as she stumbled through the door.

Downstairs Pollyanna found the doctor waiting in his gig.

"I've prescribed you for a patient, and he's sent me to get the prescription filled," announced the doctor. "It's Mr. John Pendleton. He would like to see you today, if you'll be so good as to come. Will you come? I'll bring you back before six o'clock."

"I'd love to!" exclaimed Pollyanna. "Let me ask Aunt Polly."

In a few moments she returned, hat in hand, but with rather a sober face.

"Didn't your aunt want you to go?" asked the doctor, as they drove away.

"Y-yes," sighed Pollyanna. "She—she wanted me to go *too* much, I'm afraid."

"Wanted you to go *too much!*"

Pollyanna sighed again.

"Yes. She said, 'Yes, yes, run along—do! I wish you'd gone before.'"

The doctor smiled—but with his lips only. His eyes were very grave. For some time he said nothing; then, a little hesitatingly, he asked:

"Wasn't it—your aunt I saw with you a few minutes ago?"

Pollyanna drew a long breath.

"Yes. That's what's the whole trouble, I suppose. You see, I'd dressed her up in a perfectly lovely lace shawl, and fixed her hair and put on a rose, and she looked so pretty. Didn't *you* think she looked just lovely?"

For a moment the doctor did not answer. When he did speak, his voice was low.

"Yes, Pollyanna, I—I thought she did look —just lovely."

"Did you? I'm so glad! I'll tell her," nodded the little girl, contentedly.

To her surprise the doctor gave a sudden exclamation.

"Never! Pollyanna, I—I'm afraid I shall have to ask you not to tell her—that."

"Why, Dr. Chilton! Why not? I should think you'd be glad—"

"But she might not be," cut in the doctor.

Pollyanna considered this for a moment.

"That's so—maybe she wouldn't," she sighed. "I remember now; 'twas 'cause she saw you that she ran. And she—she spoke afterwards about her being seen in that rig."

"I thought as much," declared the doctor, under his breath.

"Still, I don't see why," maintained Pollyanna, "when she looked so pretty!"

"JUST LIKE A BOOK"

JOHN PENDLETON greeted Pollyanna to-day with a smile.

"Well, Miss Pollyanna, I'm thinking you must be a very forgiving little person. I was pretty cross with you, I'm afraid, both the other day when you so kindly brought me the jelly, and that time when you found me with the broken leg. I do thank you, however; and I consider you a very brave little girl to do what you did that day. I thank you for the jelly, too," he added in a lighter voice.

"Did you like it?" asked Pollyanna with interest.

"Very much. Listen! Out in the library—

the big room where the telephone is, you know—you will find a carved box on the lower shelf of the big case with glass doors in the corner not far from the fireplace. You may bring it to me. It is not too heavy for you to carry, I think."

"Oh, I'm awfully strong," declared Pollyanna, cheerfully, as she sprang to her feet. In a minute she had returned with the box.

It was a wonderful half-hour that Pollyanna spent then. The box was full of treasures—curios that John Pendleton had picked up in years of travel—and concerning each there was some entertaining story.

The visit, certainly, was a delightful one. Before it was over, they were talking of Nancy, of Aunt Polly, and of Pollyanna's daily life.

Not until it was nearly time for her to go, did the man say, in a voice Pollyanna had never before heard from stern John Pendleton:

"Little girl, I want you to come to see me often. I thought, at first, after I found out who you were, the other day, that I didn't want you to come any more. You reminded me of—of something I have tried for long years to forget. But after a time I found I was wanting to see you so much that—that it was making me remember the thing I was so wanting to forget. So now I want you to come. Will you?"

"Why, yes, Mr. Pendleton," breathed Pollyanna. "I'd love to come!"

"Thank you," said John Pendleton, gently.

After supper that evening, Pollyanna told Nancy all about Mr. John Pendleton's wonderful carved box, and the still more wonderful things it contained.

"And ter think," sighed Nancy, "that he *showed* ye all them things, and told ye about 'em like that. He ain't the sort o' man what gen'rally takes ter kids; he ain't, he ain't."

Pollyanna smiled happily.

"But he did, Nancy," she nodded, "only I reckon even he didn't want to—*all* the time. Why, only today he owned up that one time he just felt he never wanted to see me again, because I reminded him of something he wanted to forget. But afterwards—"

"What's that?" interrupted Nancy, excitedly. "He said you reminded him of something he wanted to forget?"

"Yes. But afterwards—"

"What was it?" Nancy was eagerly insistent.

"He didn't tell me. He just said it was something."

"*The mystery!*" breathed Nancy, in an awestruck voice. "That's why he took to you in the first place. Oh, Miss Pollyanna! Why, that's just like a book—I've read lots of 'em. All of 'em had mysteries and things just like this. My stars and stockings! Just think of havin' a book lived right under yer nose like this! No wonder he took ter you; no wonder —no wonder!"

"But he didn't," cried Pollyanna, "not till *I* talked to *him*, first. And he didn't even know who I was till I took the calf's-foot jelly, and had to make him understand that Aunt Polly didn't send it, and—"

Nancy sprang to her feet and clasped her hands together suddenly.

"Oh, Miss Pollyanna, I know—I *know* I know!" she exulted rapturously. The next minute she was down at Pollyanna's side again. "It was after he found out you was Miss Polly's niece that he said he didn't ever want ter see ye again, wa'n't it?"

"Oh, yes. I told him that the last time I saw him, and he told me this today."

"I thought as much," triumphed Nancy. "And Miss Polly wouldn't send the jelly herself, would she?"

"No."

"And you told him she didn't send it?"

"Why, yes. I—"

"And he began ter act queer and cry out sudden after he found out you was her niece. He did that, didn't he?"

"Why, y-yes. He did act a little queer—over that jelly," admitted Pollyanna, with a thoughtful frown.

Nancy drew a long sigh.

"Then I've got it, sure! Now listen. *John Pendleton and Miss Polly were sweethearts!*"

"Why, Nancy, that couldn't be! She doesn't like him," objected Pollyanna.

Nancy gave her a scornful glance.

"Of course she don't! *That's* the quarrel! It's like this. Just before you come, Mr. Tom told me Miss Polly had had a sweetheart once. I didn't believe it. But Mr. Tom said she had, and that he was livin' right in this town. And *now* I know, of course. It's John Pendleton. Hain't he got a mystery in his life? Hain't he owned up that you remind him of somethin' he wants ter forget? Just as if *anybody* couldn't see 'twas Miss Polly! An' her sayin' she wouldn't send him no jelly, too. Why, Miss Pollyanna, it's as plain as the nose on yer face; it is, it is!"

"Oh-h!" breathed Pollyanna, in wide-eyed amazement. "But I should think if they loved each other, they'd be glad to make up!"

Nancy sniffed disdainfully.

"If there *is* a set o' folks in the world that wouldn't have no use for that 'ere 'glad game' o' your'n, it'd be a pair o' quarrelin' lovers; and that's what they be. I ain't sayin', though, but what it would be a pretty slick piece of business if you could *get* 'em ter play it—so they *would* be glad ter make up!"

PRISMS

IT WAS toward the end of August that Pollyanna, making an early morning call on John Pendleton, found the flaming band of blue and gold and green edged with red and violet lying across his pillow.

"Why, Mr. Pendleton, it's a baby rainbow —come in to pay you a visit!" she exclaimed, clapping her hands together softly. "But how *did* it get in?" she cried.

"Well, I suppose it 'got in' through the bevelled edge of that glass thermometer in the window," John Pendleton said.

"It's so pretty! And does just the sun do that? My, if it was mine, I'd have it hang in the sun all day long!"

"Lots of good you'd get out of the thermometer, then," laughed the man.

He was watching Pollyanna's face a little curiously. Suddenly a new thought came to him. He turned smiling eyes toward the wondering Pollyanna.

"Bring me the candlestick, please."

With both hands she brought it; and in a moment he was slipping off the prism pendants, one by one, until they lay, a dozen of them, side by side, on the bed.

"Now, my dear, suppose you take them and hook them to that little string fixed across the window. If you really *want* to live in a rainbow—we'll have to have a rainbow for you to live in!"

Pollyanna had not hung up three of the

pendants in the sunlit window before she saw a little of what was going to happen. At last her task was finished, and she stepped back with a cry of delight. The wall, the floor, and the furniture, even to the bed itself, were aflame with shimmering bits of color.

"Oh, oh, oh, how lovely!" breathed Pollyanna. Then she laughed suddenly. "I just reckon the sun is trying to play the game now, don't you? Oh, I forgot. You don't know about the game."

"Suppose you tell me, then."

And this time Pollyanna told him. She told him the whole thing from the very first—from the crutches that should have been a doll. As she talked, she did not look at his face. Her rapt eyes were still on the dancing flecks of color.

"And that's all," she sighed, when she had finished. "Now you know why I said the sun was trying to play it—that game."

For a moment there was silence. Then a low voice from the bed said unsteadily:

"Perhaps. But I'm thinking that the finest prism of them all is you, Pollyanna."

Pollyanna, looking into his face, wondered why there were tears in his eyes.

A SURPRISE

POLLYANNA entered school in September. She was soon a happy member of a class of girls and boys her own age.

Pollyanna did not forget her old friends. True, she could not give them quite so much time now, but she gave them what time she could. Perhaps John Pendleton, of them all, however, was the most dissatisfied.

One Saturday afternoon he spoke to her.

"See here, Pollyanna, how would you like to come and live with me?" he asked. "I don't see anything of you, nowadays."

"I thought you didn't like to have folks 'round," she said.

"Oh, but that was before you taught me to play that wonderful game of yours. That's why I want you to help me play it."

"Mr. Pendleton, you don't really mean—that?"

"But I do. I want you. Will you come?"

"Why, Mr. Pendleton, I can't—you know I can't. Aunt Polly has been so good to me, and she took me when I didn't have anybody left but the Ladies' Aid and—"

"Pollyanna, long years ago I loved somebody very much. I hoped to bring her, some day, to this house. I pictured how happy we'd be together in our home all the long years to come."

"Yes," pitied Pollyanna, her eyes shining with sympathy.

"But—well, I didn't bring her here. I just didn't—that's all. And ever since then this great gray pile of stone has been a house—never a home. It takes a woman's hand and heart, or a child's presence, to make a home, Pollyanna; and I have not had either."

"Mr. Pendleton, you—you mean that you wish you—you had had that woman's hand and heart all this time?"

"Why, y-yes, Pollyanna."

"Oh, I'm so glad! Then it's all right," sighed the little girl. "Now you can take us both, and everything will be lovely. Aunt

Polly isn't won over, yet; but I'm sure she will be if you tell it to her just as you did to me, and then we'd both come, of course."

A look of terror leaped to the man's eyes.

"Aunt Polly come—*here!*"

Pollyanna's eyes widened a little.

"Would you rather go *there?*" she asked. "You said it was here that you had wanted Aunt Polly's hand and heart all these years to make a home, and—"

A cry came from the man's throat.

"Pollyanna, for Heaven's sake, say nothing of what I asked you—yet," he begged, in a low voice.

Pollyanna dimpled into a sunny smile.

"Of course not! Just as if I didn't know you'd rather tell her yourself!" she called back merrily over her shoulder.

John Pendleton fell limply in his chair.

"Why, what's up?" demanded the doctor, a minute later, his fingers on his patient's galloping pulse.

A whimsical smile trembled on John Pendleton's lips.

"Overdose of your—tonic, I guess," he laughed, as he noted the doctor's eyes following Pollyanna's figure down the driveway.

ANOTHER SURPRISE

POLLYANNA found a very nervous John Pendleton waiting for her the next day.

"Pollyanna," he began at once. "I've been trying all night to puzzle out what you meant by all that, yesterday—about my wanting your Aunt Polly's hand and heart here all those years. What did you mean?"

"Why, because you both loved each other once, and I was glad you still felt that way."

"Your Aunt Polly—and I?"

At the obvious surprise in the man's voice, Pollyanna opened her eyes wide.

"Why, Mr. Pendleton, Nancy said—"

The man gave a short little laugh.

"Indeed! Well, I'm afraid I shall have to say that Nancy—didn't know."

"Oh, dear! And it was all going so splendidly," almost sobbed Pollyanna. "I'd have been so glad to come—with Aunt Polly."

"And you won't—now?"

"Of course not! I'm Aunt Polly's."

The man turned now, almost fiercely.

"Before you were hers, Pollyanna, you were—your mother's. And—it was your mother's hand and heart that I wanted."

"My mother's!"

"Yes. I had not meant to tell you, but perhaps it's better, after all, that I do—now." John Pendleton's face had grown very white. Pollyanna, her eyes wide and frightened, and her lips parted, was gazing at him fixedly. "I loved your mother; but she—didn't love me. And after a time she went away with—your father. I did not know until then how much I did care. Then, one day, you danced into my life. I found out who you were, and I thought then I never wanted to see you again. I didn't want to be reminded of—your mother. But you know how that came out. And now I want you always."

The little girl's forehead puckered into a wistful frown.

"Aunt Polly has been so good to me," she

began; but the man interrupted her sharply.

"Of course she's been good to you! But she doesn't want you half so much as I do."

"Why, Mr. Pendleton, she's glad, I know, to have—"

"Glad!" interrupted the man, thoroughly losing his patience now. "I'll wager Miss Polly doesn't know how to be glad—for anything! Oh, she does her duty, I know. She's a very *dutiful* woman. But I know her. You just ask her and see if she won't let you come."

Pollyanna rose to her feet with a long sigh.

"All right. I'll ask her," she said wistfully. There was a moment's silence. Then she added: "Well, anyhow, I'm glad I didn't tell her yesterday—'cause then I supposed *she* was wanted, too."

"Well, yes, Pollyanna. I guess it is just as well you didn't mention it—yesterday."

"I didn't—only to the doctor; and of course he doesn't count."

"The doctor!" cried John Pendleton, turning quickly. "Not—Dr.—Chilton?"

"Yes."

"Well, of all the—" muttered the man, falling back in his chair. And Pollyanna wondered why he gave that queer little laugh.

A QUESTION ANSWERED

THE SKY was darkening fast with what appeared to be an approaching shower when Pollyanna hurried down the hill from John Pendleton's house. Halfway home she met Nancy with an umbrella. By that time, however, the clouds had shifted position.

"Guess it's goin' 'round ter the north," announced Nancy, eyeing the sky. "I thought 'twas, all the time, but Miss Polly wanted me ter come with this. She was *worried* about ye! She's at last gettin' down somewheres near human—like folks; an' she ain't jest doin' her duty by ye all the time."

"Why, Nancy, Aunt Polly always does her duty. She—she's a very dutiful woman!" Unconsciously Pollyanna repeated John Pendleton's words of half an hour before.

Nancy chuckled.

"You're right she is—and she always was, I guess! But she's somethin' more, now, since you came."

Pollyanna's face changed. Her brows drew into a troubled frown.

"There, that's what I was going to ask you, Nancy," she sighed. "Do you think Aunt Polly likes to have me here?"

"Likes ter have ye here?" cried Nancy, indignantly. "As if that wa'n't jest what I was tellin' of ye! Didn't she send me posthaste with an umbrella 'cause she see a little cloud in the sky? Didn't she make me tote yer things all downstairs, so you could have the pretty room you wanted? Why, Miss Pollyanna, there ain't no tellin' how she'd miss ye —if ye wa'n't here."

"As if I'd leave her now!" thought Pollyanna, as she climbed the stairs to her room a little later.

The task of telling John Pendleton of her decision would not be an easy one, Pollyanna knew, and she dreaded it. She was sorry for the long, lonely life that had made him so unhappy. She wished that somewhere, someone might be found who— And it was at this point that a thought came to her.

As soon as she could, after that, she hurried to John Pendleton's house, and in due time she found herself in the great library.

"Well, Pollyanna, is it to be the 'glad game' with me?" asked the man gently.

"Oh, yes," cried Pollyanna. "I've thought of the very gladdest kind of a thing."

"With—*you?*" asked John Pendleton.

"No, but—"

"Pollyanna, you aren't going to say no!"

"I—I've got to, Mr. Pendleton; truly I have. Aunt Polly—"

"Did she *refuse*—to let you—come?"

"I—I didn't ask her," stammered the little girl, miserably. "You see, I found out—without asking. Aunt Polly *wants* me with her, and—and I want to stay, too. You don't know how good she's been to me. Oh, I *couldn't* leave Aunt Polly—now!"

There was a long pause. Only the snapping of the wood fire in the grate broke the silence. At last, however, the man spoke.

"No, Pollyanna; I see. You couldn't leave her—now," he said. "I won't ask you—again." The last word was so low it was almost inaudible; but Pollyanna heard.

"Oh, but you don't know about the rest of it," she reminded him eagerly. "There's the very gladdest thing you *can* do—truly there is! You said only a—a woman's hand and heart or a child's presence could make a home. And I can get it for you—a child's presence. Not me, you know, but another one."

"As if I would have any but you!"

"But you will—when you know; you're so kind and good! Why, think of the prisms and that money you save for heathen, and—"

"Pollyanna!" interrupted the man, savagely. "Once for all let us end that nonsense! There *is* no money for the heathen. I never sent a penny to them in my life. There!"

He lifted his chin and braced himself to meet what he expected—the grieved disappointment of Pollyanna's eyes. To his amazement, however, there was only surprised joy.

"Oh, oh!" she cried, clapping her hands. "I'm so glad! That is," she corrected, "I don't mean that I'm not sorry for the heathen, only just now I can't help being glad that you don't want the little India boys, because all the rest have wanted them. And so I'm glad you'd rather have Jimmy Bean. Now I know you'll take him!"

"Take—*who?*"

"Jimmy Bean. He's the 'child's presence,' you know; and he'll be so glad to be it. I had to tell him last week that even my Ladies' Aid out West wouldn't take him, and he was so disappointed. But now—when he hears of this—he'll be so glad!"

"Will he? Well, I won't," ejaculated the man, decisively.

"You don't mean—you won't take him?"

"I certainly do mean just that."

"But he'd be a lovely child's presence," faltered Pollyanna. She was almost crying now. "Maybe you think a nice live little boy wouldn't be better than that old dead skeleton you keep somewhere, but I think it would!"

"*Skeleton?*"

"Yes. Nancy said you had one in your closet, somewhere."

"Why, what—" Suddenly the man threw back his head and laughed. He laughed so heartily that Pollyanna began to cry from pure nervousness. When he saw that, John Pendleton sat erect very promptly.

"Pollyanna, I suspect you are right," he said gently. "In fact, I *know* that a 'nice live little boy' would be far better than—my skeleton in the closet; only—we aren't always willing to make the exchange. We are apt to still cling to—our skeletons, Pollyanna. However, suppose you tell me a little more about this nice little boy." And Pollyanna told him.

Perhaps the laugh cleared the air. At all events, when Pollyanna went home that night she carried with her an invitation for Jimmy Bean himself to call at the great house with Pollyanna the next Saturday afternoon.

AN ACCIDENT

AT MRS. SNOW'S request, Pollyanna went one day to Dr. Chilton's office to get the name of a medicine.

"I've never been to your home before! This *is* your home, isn't it?" Pollyanna asked.

The doctor smiled a little sadly.

"Yes—such as 'tis," he answered. "But they're just rooms, that's all."

Pollyanna nodded her head wisely.

"I know. It takes a woman's hand and heart, or a child's presence to make a home."

"Eh?" The doctor wheeled about abruptly.

"Mr. Pendleton told me," nodded Polly-anna, "about the woman's hand and heart, or the child's presence, you know. He says his is just a house, too. Oh—and I forgot to tell you. It wasn't Aunt Polly that Mr. Pendleton loved long ago. You see, I told you it was —but I made a mistake. I hope *you* didn't tell anyone," she finished anxiously.

"No—I didn't tell anyone, Pollyanna."

"Oh, that's all right, then," sighed Pollyanna in relief. "You see, you're the only one I told, and I thought Mr. Pendleton looked sort of funny when I said I'd told *you*."

"Did he?" The doctor's lips twitched.

"Yes. And of course he wouldn't want many people to know it—when 'twasn't true. But why don't you get a woman's hand and heart, Dr. Chilton?"

There was a moment's silence. Then, very gravely, the doctor said, "They're not always to be had—for the asking."

Pollyanna's eyes widened in surprise.

"Dr. Chilton, you don't mean—you didn't try to get somebody's hand and heart once, like Mr. Pendleton, and couldn't, did you?"

The doctor got to his feet.

"There, there, Pollyanna, never mind about that. Run back now to Mrs. Snow. I've written down the name of the medicine, and directions on how she is to take it."

It was on the last day of October that the accident occurred. Pollyanna, hurrying home from school, crossed the road at an apparently safe distance in front of a swiftly approaching car.

Just what happened, no one could seem to tell afterward. Neither was there anyone found who could tell why it happened or who was to blame that it did happen. There appeared to be no bones broken, and the cut was of slight consequence, but Dr. Warren had looked very grave, had shaken his head slowly, and had said that time alone could tell. The patient had not fully recovered consciousness, but at present she seemed to be resting as comfortably as could be expected. A trained nurse had been sent for, and would come that night. That was all.

It was sometime during the next morning that Pollyanna opened her eyes.

"Why, Aunt Polly, what's the matter? Isn't it daytime? Why don't I get up?" she cried.

"No, dear, I wouldn't try—just yet," soothed her aunt quickly, but very quietly.

"But what is the matter? Why can't I get up?"

Miss Polly cleared her throat and tried to swallow the lump that would scarcely let her speak.

"You were hurt, dear, by the automobile last night. But never mind that now. Auntie wants you to rest and go to sleep again."

"Hurt? Oh, yes; I—I ran." Pollyanna's eyes were dazed. She lifted her hand to her forehead. "Why, it's—done up, and it—hurts!"

"Yes, dear, but never mind. Just rest."

"But, Aunt Polly, I feel so funny, and so bad! My legs feel so—so queer—only they don't *feel*—at all!"

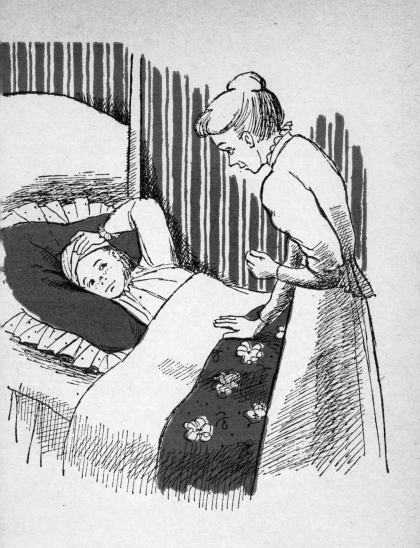

JOHN PENDLETON

POLLYANNA did not realize anything very clearly until a week had passed. Then she had to be told all over again what had occurred.

"And so it's hurt that I am, and not sick," she sighed at last. "Well, I'm glad of that. I'd so much rather have broken legs like Mr. Pendleton's than life-long-invalids like Mrs. Snow, you know. Broken legs get well, and life-long-invalids don't."

Miss Polly—who had said nothing whatever about broken legs—got suddenly to her feet and walked to the little dressing table across the room. Her face was white and drawn.

On the bed Pollyanna lay blinking at the dancing band of colors on the ceiling, which came from one of the prisms in the window.

"I'm glad it isn't smallpox that ails me, too," she murmured contentedly. "That would be worse than freckles. I'm so glad Mr. Pendleton gave me those prisms! I'm glad of some things I haven't said yet. I don't know but I'm 'most glad I was hurt."

"Pollyanna!"

Pollyanna laughed softly again. "Well, you see, since I have been hurt, you've called me 'dear' lots of times—and you didn't before. I love to be called 'dear'—by folks that belong to you, I mean. Some of the Ladies' Aiders did call me that; and of course that was pretty nice, but not so nice as if they had belonged to me, like you do. Oh, Aunt Polly, I'm so glad you belong to me!"

Aunt Polly did not answer. Her eyes were full of tears. She had turned away and was hurrying from the room through the door by which the nurse had just entered.

It was that afternoon that Nancy ran out to Old Tom, who was cleaning harnesses in the barn.

"Mr. Tom," she panted, "who do you s'pose is in the parlor now with the mistress? Who, I say?"

Old Tom shook his head.

"There's no tellin'," he declared.

"Yes, there is. I'm tellin'. It's—John Pendleton! Jest think, Mr. Tom—*him* a-callin' on *her!*—him, what she hain't spoke to for years! But I let him in an' went an' told her."

"What did she say?" Old Tom held his breath suspended.

"Nothin'—at first. She was so still I thought she hadn't heard; and I was jest goin' ter say it over when she speaks up quiet like: 'Tell Mr. Pendleton I will be down at once.' An' I come an' told him. Then I come out here an' told you," finished Nancy.

"Humph!" grunted Old Tom; and fell to work again.

In the ceremonious "parlor" of the Harrington homestead, Mr. John Pendleton did not have to wait long before a swift step warned him of Miss Polly's coming.

"I called to ask for—Pollyanna," he began at once, a little brusquely.

"Thank you. She is about the same," said Miss Polly. "Dr. Warren himself seems—at sea. He is in correspondence now with a New York specialist. They have arranged for a consultation."

"But—but what *were* her injuries that you do know?"

"A slight cut on the head, one or two bruises, and—and an injury to the spine which has seemed to cause—paralysis from the hips down."

A low cry came from the man. There was a brief silence; then, huskily, he asked:

"And Pollyanna—how does she—take it?"

"She knows she can't—move; but she thinks her legs are—broken. She says she's glad it's broken legs like yours rather than 'life-long-invalids' like Mrs. Snow's, because broken legs get well, and the other—doesn't.

She talks like that all the time, until it—it seems as if I should—die!"

Through the blur of tears in his own eyes, the man saw the drawn face opposite, twisted with emotion. Involuntarily his thoughts went back to what Pollyanna had said when he had made his final plea for her presence: "Oh, I *couldn't* leave Aunt Polly—now!"

It was this thought that made him ask very gently, as soon as he could control his voice:

"I wonder if you know, Miss Harrington, how hard I tried to get Pollyanna to come and live with me. I wanted to adopt her—legally, you understand; making her my heir. But she would not leave you. She said you had been so good to her. She wanted to stay with you—and she said she *thought* you wanted her to stay," he finished.

He did not look toward Miss Polly. But instantly he heard a swift step at his side, and found a shaking hand thrust toward him.

"When the specialist comes, and I know anything definite about Pollyanna, I will let you hear from me," said a trembling voice. "Good-by—and thank you for coming. Pollyanna will be—pleased."

A WAITING GAME

O N THE DAY after John Pendleton's call at the Harrington homestead, Miss Polly set herself to the task of preparing Pollyanna for the visit of the specialist.

"Pollyanna, my dear," she began gently, "we have decided that we want another doctor besides Dr. Warren to see you. Another one might tell us something new to do—to help you get well faster, you know."

A joyous light came to Pollyanna's face. "Dr. Chilton! Oh, Aunt Polly, I'd so love to

have Dr. Chilton! I've wanted him all the
time, but I was afraid you didn't, on account
of his seeing you in the sun parlor that day,
you know; so I didn't like to say anything.
But I'm so glad you do want him!"

Aunt Polly's face had turned white, then
red, then back to white again. But when she
answered, she showed very plainly that she
was trying to speak lightly and cheerfully.

"Oh, no, dear! It wasn't Dr. Chilton at all
that I meant. It is a new doctor—a very famous doctor from New York, who—who knows
a great deal about—about hurts like yours."

Pollyanna's face fell.

"I don't believe he knows half so much as
Dr. Chilton."

"Oh, yes, he does, I'm sure, dear."

"But it was Dr. Chilton who doctored Mr.
Pendleton's broken leg, Aunt Polly. If—if
you don't mind *very* much, I *would like* to
have Dr. Chilton—truly I would!"

The nurse entered the room at that moment, and Aunt Polly rose to her feet
abruptly, a look of relief on her face.

"I am very sorry, Pollyanna," she said, a
little stiffly, "but I'm afraid you'll have to let
me be the judge, this time."

A DOOR AJAR

DR. MEAD, the specialist, was a tall, broad-shouldered man with kind gray eyes, and a cheerful smile. Pollyanna liked him at once, and told him so.

"You look quite a lot like *my* doctor, you see," she added engagingly.

"*Your* doctor?" Dr. Mead glanced in evident surprise at Dr. Warren, talking with the nurse a few feet away. Dr. Warren was a small man with a pointed brown beard.

"Oh, *that* isn't my doctor," smiled Pollyanna. "Dr. Warren is Aunt Polly's doctor. My doctor is Dr. Chilton. You see, *I* wanted Dr. Chilton all the time, but Aunt Polly wanted you. She said you knew more than Dr. Chilton—about broken legs like mine. If you do, I can be glad for that. Do you?"

A swift something crossed the doctor's face that Pollyanna could not quite translate.

"Only time can tell that, little girl," he said gently.

Everyone said afterward that it was the cat that did it. Certainly, if Fluffy had not poked an insistent paw and nose against Pollyanna's unlatched door, the door would not have swung noiselessly open on its hinges until it stood perhaps a foot ajar; and if the door had not been open, Pollyanna would not have heard her aunt's words.

In the hall the two doctors, the nurse, and Miss Polly stood talking. In Pollyanna's room Fluffy had just jumped to the bed with a little purring "meow" of joy when through the open door sounded clearly and sharply Aunt Polly's agonized exclamation.

"Not that! Doctor, not that! You don't mean—the child—will *never walk* again!"

It was all confusion then. First, from the bedroom came Pollyanna's terrified "Aunt Polly—Aunt Polly!" Then Miss Polly, seeing the open door and realizing that her words had been heard, gave a low little moan and—for the first time in her life—fainted dead away.

The nurse, with a choking "She heard!" stumbled toward the open door. The two doctors stayed with Miss Polly.

In Pollyanna's room, the nurse found a

purring gray cat on the bed vainly trying to attract the attention of a white-faced, wild-eyed little girl.

"Miss Hunt, please, I want Aunt Polly. I want her right away, quick, please! I want her to tell me 'tisn't true—'tisn't true!"

The nurse tried to speak, but no words came. Something in her face sent an added terror to Pollyanna's eyes.

"Miss Hunt, you *did* hear her! It *is* true! Oh, it *isn't* true! You don't mean I can't ever —walk again?"

"There, there, dear—don't, don't!" choked the nurse. "Perhaps he didn't know. Perhaps he was mistaken. All doctors make mistakes sometimes. Just—just don't think any more about it now—please don't, dear."

Pollyanna flung out her arms wildly.

"But I can't help thinking about it," she sobbed. "It's all there is now to think about. Why, Miss Hunt, how am I going to school, or to see Mr. Pendleton, or Mrs. Snow, or— or anybody?" She caught her breath and sobbed wildly for a moment. Suddenly she stopped and looked up, a new terror in her eyes. "Why, Miss Hunt, if I can't walk, how am I ever going to be glad for—*anything?*"

TWO VISITS

IT WAS Nancy who was sent to tell Mr. John Pendleton of Dr. Mead's verdict. Miss Polly had remembered her promise to let him have direct information from the house.

"I'm Nancy, sir," she said respectfully, in response to the surprised questioning of his eyes, when he came into the room. "Miss Harrington sent me to tell you about—Miss Pollyanna."

"Well?"

"It ain't well," she choked. "The doctor says she can't walk again—never."

For a moment there was absolute silence in the room. Then the man spoke, in a voice shaken with emotion.

"Poor—little—girl! Poor—little—girl!"

Nancy glanced at him. She had not supposed that sour, cross, stern John Pendleton could look like that. In a moment he spoke again, still in the low, unsteady voice.

"She herself doesn't know yet—of course —does she?"

"But she does, sir," sobbed Nancy, "an' that's what makes it all the harder. She found out—drat that cat! I begs yer pardon," apologized the girl, hurriedly. "It's only that the cat pushed open the door an' Miss Pollyanna overheard 'em talkin'. She found out—that way."

"Poor—little—girl!" sighed the man again.

"Yes, sir. You'd say so, sir, if you could see her," choked Nancy. "She keeps thinkin' all the time of new things she can't do—*now*. It worries her, too, 'cause she can't seem ter be glad—maybe you don't know about her game, though."

"The 'glad game'?" asked the man. "Oh, yes, she told me of that."

"Then I tried ter remind her how she used ter say the game was all the nicer ter play when—when it was hard," resumed Nancy. "But she says that, too, is diff'rent—when it really *is* hard. An' I must be goin', now, sir," she broke off abruptly.

It did not take long for the entire town to learn that the great New York doctor had said Pollyanna Whittier would never walk again; and certainly never before had the town been so stirred. It seemed unbelievable, impossible, cruel.

At all events, almost at once, the mistress of the Harrington homestead, greatly to her surprise, began to receive calls from people —many of whom Miss Polly had not supposed that her niece knew at all.

Some came in and sat down for a stiff five or ten minutes. Some brought a book, flowers, or a dainty to tempt the palate. Some cried frankly. But all inquired very anxiously for the little injured girl.

First came Mr. John Pendleton. He came without his crutches today.

"I don't need to tell you how shocked I am," he began. "Can nothing be done?"

Miss Polly gave a gesture of despair.

"Oh, we're 'doing,' of course, all the time. Dr. Mead prescribed certain treatments and medicines that might help, and Dr. Warren is carrying them out to the letter. But—Dr. Mead held out almost no hope."

John Pendleton rose abruptly—though he had but just come. His face was white, and his mouth was set into stern lines.

"I have a message for Pollyanna," he said. "Will you tell her, please, that I have seen Jimmy Bean and—that he's going to be my

boy hereafter. Tell her I thought she would be—*glad* to know. I shall adopt him, probably. I think Pollyanna will understand. You will tell her I thought she would be—*glad?*"

"Why, of—of course," faltered Miss Polly.

"Thank you," bowed John Pendleton, as he turned to go.

With a somewhat dazed face Miss Polly went upstairs to Pollyanna's room.

"Pollyanna, I have a message for you from Mr. John Pendleton. He has just been here. He says to tell you he has taken Jimmy Bean for his little boy. He said he thought you'd be glad to know it."

Pollyanna's wistful little face flamed into sudden joy.

"Glad? *Glad?* Well, I reckon I am glad! Oh, Aunt Polly, I've so wanted to find a place for Jimmy—and that's such a lovely place! Besides, I'm so glad for Mr. Pendleton, too. You see, now he'll have the child's presence."

"The—what?"

"The child's presence," stammered Pollyanna, hastily. "Mr. Pendleton told me once, you see, that only a woman's hand and heart or a child's presence could make a—a home. And now he's got it—the child's presence."

"Oh, I—see," said Miss Polly very gently; and she did—more than Pollyanna realized.

"Dr. Chilton says so, too—that it takes a woman's hand and heart, or a child's presence, to make a home, you know."

Miss Polly turned with a start.

"*Dr. Chilton!* How do you know—that?"

"He told me so. 'Twas when he said he lived in just rooms, you know—not a home."

Miss Polly did not answer.

"So I asked him why he didn't get 'em—a woman's hand and heart, and have a home. Then he said very low that you couldn't always get 'em for the asking."

There was a brief silence. Miss Polly's cheeks were unnaturally pink.

Pollyanna sighed.

"He wants one, anyhow, I know, and I wish he could have one. Because, on another day, he said something else. He said that he'd give all the world if he did have one woman's hand and heart. Why, Aunt Polly, what's the matter?" Aunt Polly had risen hurriedly and gone to the window.

"Nothing, dear. I was changing the position of this prism," said Aunt Polly, whose whole face now was aflame.

THE GAME AND ITS PLAYERS

"NANCY!"

Miss Polly spoke sharply. The series of puzzling, disconcerting visits of the last few days had strained her nerves to the snapping point.

"Nancy, *will* you tell me what this absurd 'game' is that the whole town seems to be babbling about? And what, please, has my niece to do with it? *Why* does everybody send word to her that they're 'playing it'? As near as I can judge, half the town are putting on blue ribbons, or stopping family quarrels, or learning to like something they never liked before, and all because of Pollyanna."

To Miss Polly's surprise and dismay, Nancy burst into tears.

"It means that ever since last June that blessed child has jest been makin' the whole town glad, an' now they're turnin' 'round an' tryin' ter make her a little glad, too."

"Glad of what?"

"Just glad! That's the game."

Miss Polly actually stamped her foot.

"There you go like all the rest, Nancy. *What* game?"

"I'll tell ye, ma'am. It's a game Miss Pollyanna's father learned her ter play. She got a pair of crutches once in a missionary barrel when she was wantin' a doll; an' she cried, of course, like any child would. It seems 'twas then her father told her that there wasn't ever anythin' but what there was somethin' about it that you could be glad about; an' that she could be glad about them crutches."

"Glad for—*crutches!*" Miss Polly choked back a sob. She was thinking of the helpless little legs on the bed upstairs.

"Yes'm. That's what I said, an' Miss Pollyanna said that's what *she* said, too. But he

told her she *could* be glad—'cause she *didn't need 'em*."

"Oh-h!" cried Miss Polly.

"And after that she said he made a regular game of it—findin' somethin' in everythin' ter be glad about. An' she said ye could do it, too, and that ye didn't seem ter mind not havin' the doll so much, 'cause ye was so glad ye *didn't* need the crutches. An' they called it the 'jest bein' glad' game."

"But why hasn't—she told me—the game?" faltered Miss Polly.

"Beggin' yer pardon, ma'am, you told her not ter speak of—her father; so she couldn't tell ye. 'Twas her father's game, ye see."

Miss Polly bit her lip.

"She wanted ter tell ye, first off," continued

Nancy, a little unsteadily. "She wanted somebody ter play it with, ye know."

"Well, I know somebody who'll play it—now," choked Miss Polly, as she turned and sped through the kitchen doorway.

Behind her, Nancy stood staring amazedly.

"Well, I'll believe anythin'—anythin' now," she muttered to herself.

A little later, in Pollyanna's room, the nurse left Miss Polly and Pollyanna alone together. Miss Polly sternly forced her voice to be cheerfully matter-of-fact. "Nancy told me about your beautiful game. I'm going to play it now—with you."

"Oh, Aunt Polly—*you?* I'm so glad!"

Aunt Polly caught her breath a little sharply. It was even harder this time to keep her voice steady, but she did it.

"Yes, dear; and there are all those others, too. The whole town is playing the game, and the whole town is wonderfully happier—all because of one little girl who taught the people a new game."

Pollyanna clapped her hands.

"Why, Aunt Polly, there *is* something I can be glad about. I can be glad I've *had* my legs—else I couldn't have done that!"

THROUGH AN OPEN
WINDOW

ONE by one the short winter days came
and went—but they were not short to
Pollyanna. They were long, and sometimes
full of pain. Pollyanna now, like Mrs. Snow,
was knitting wonderful things out of bright
colored worsteds and it made Pollyanna—
again like Mrs. Snow—so glad she had her
hands and arms, anyway.

The winter passed, and spring came. Anxious watchers over Pollyanna's condition could see little change. There seemed every reason to believe, indeed, that Dr. Mead's worst fears would be realized—that Pollyanna would never walk again.

Beldingsville, of course, kept itself informed concerning Pollyanna; and of Beldingsville, one man in particular fumed and fretted himself into a fever of anxiety. In the end, Mr. John Pendleton, somewhat to his surprise, received one Saturday morning a call from Dr. Thomas Chilton.

"Pendleton," began the doctor, abruptly, "I want to see that child. I want to make an examination. I simply *must* make an examination."

"Well—can't you?"

"*Can't* I! Pendleton, you know very well I haven't been inside that door for more than fifteen years. You don't know—but I will tell you—that the mistress of that house told me that the *next* time she *asked* me to enter it, I might take it that she was begging my pardon, and that all would be as before— which meant that she'd marry me. Perhaps you see her summoning me, but I don't!"

"But couldn't you go—without a summons?"

The doctor frowned.

"Well, hardly. *I* have some pride."

"But if you're so anxious—couldn't you swallow your pride and forget the quarrel—"

"Forget the quarrel!" interrupted the doctor, savagely. "I'm not talking of that kind of pride. I'd go from here to there on my knees if that would do any good. It's *professional* pride I'm talking about. It's a case of sickness, and I'm a doctor. I can't say, 'Here, take me!' Can I?"

"Chilton, what *was* the quarrel?" demanded Pendleton.

"Never mind the quarrel! So far as I am concerned, I am willing to say there was no quarrel. Pendleton, I must see that child. It may mean life or death. It will mean—I honestly believe—nine chances out of ten that Pollyanna Whittier will walk again!"

The words were spoken clearly, impressively; and they were spoken just as the one who uttered them had almost reached the open window near John Pendleton's chair. Jimmy Bean, at his Saturday morning task of pulling up the first little green weeds of

151

the flower beds, sat up with ears and eyes wide open.

"Walk! Pollyanna!" John Pendleton was saying. "What do you mean?"

"I mean that from what I can hear and learn—a mile from her bedside—that her case is very much like one that a college friend of mine has just helped. For years he's been making this sort of thing a special study. I've kept in touch with him, and studied, too, in a way. And from what I hear—but I want to *see* the girl! But how can I—without a direct request from her aunt?—which I'll never get!"

"She must be made to ask you! If she could be made to see—to understand," urged John Pendleton.

"Yes; and who's going to do it?" demanded the doctor, with a savage turn.

"I don't know," groaned the other, miserably.

Outside the window Jimmy Bean stirred suddenly. Up to now he had scarcely breathed, so intently had he listened to every word.

"Well, by Jinks, I know!" he whispered, exultingly. "*I'm* a-goin' ter do it!"

JIMMY TAKES THE HELM

"IT'S JIMMY BEAN. He wants ter see ye, ma'am," announced Nancy in the doorway.

"Me?" rejoined Miss Polly, plainly surprised. "Are you sure he did not mean Miss Pollyanna? He may see her a few minutes today, if he likes."

"Yes'm. I told him. But he said it was you he wanted."

"Very well, I'll come down." And Miss Polly arose from her chair a little wearily.

In the sitting room she found waiting for

her a round-eyed, flushed-faced boy, who began to speak at once.

"Ma'am, I s'pose it's dreadful—what I'm doin', an' what I'm sayin', but I can't help it. Ter begin with, Dr. Chilton come ter see Mr. Pendleton, an' they talked in the library."

"Yes, Jimmy." Miss Polly's voice was rather faint.

"Well, the window was open, and I was weedin' the flower bed under it; an' I heard 'em talk. And I'm glad I listened. You will be when I tell ye. Why, it may make Pollyanna—walk!"

"Jimmy, what do you mean?" Miss Polly was leaning forward eagerly.

"There, I told ye so," nodded Jimmy, contentedly. "Well, Dr. Chilton knows some doctor somewhere that can cure Pollyanna, he thinks—make her walk, ye know; but he can't tell sure till he *sees* her. And he wants ter see her somethin' awful, but he told Mr. Pendleton that you wouldn't let him."

Miss Polly's face turned very red.

"But, Jimmy, I—I can't—I couldn't! That is, I didn't know!" Miss Polly was twisting her fingers together helplessly.

"Yes, an' that's what I come ter tell ye

so you *would* know," asserted Jimmy, eagerly. "They said that for some reason—I didn't rightly catch what—you wouldn't let Dr. Chilton come. An' they was wishin' somebody could make you understand, only they didn't know who could; an' I was outside the winder, an' I says ter myself right away, 'By Jinks, I'll do it!' An' I come—an' have I made ye understand?"

"Yes; but, Jimmy, about that doctor," implored Miss Polly, feverishly. "Who was he? What did he do? Are they *sure* he could make Pollyanna walk?"

"I don't know who he was. They didn't say. Dr. Chilton knows him, an' he's just cured somebody just like her, Dr. Chilton thinks. Anyhow, they didn't seem ter be doin' no worryin' about *him*. 'Twas *you* they was worryin' about, 'cause you wouldn't let Dr. Chilton see her. An' say—you will let him come, won't you?"

Miss Polly turned her head from side to side. Her breath was coming in little uneven, rapid gasps. Jimmy, watching her with anxious eyes, thought she was going to cry. After a minute she said brokenly:

"Yes—I'll let—Dr. Chilton—see her."

A NEW UNCLE

THE NEXT time Dr. Warren entered the chamber where Pollyanna lay watching the dancing shimmer of color on the ceiling, a tall, broad-shouldered man followed close behind him.

"Dr. Chilton! Oh, Dr. Chilton, how glad I am to see you!" cried Pollyanna. "But of course, if Aunt Polly doesn't want—"

"It is all right, my dear; don't worry," soothed Miss Polly, hurrying forward. "I have told Dr. Chilton that—that I want him to look you over—with Dr. Warren, this morning."

"Oh, then you asked him to come," murmured Pollyanna, contentedly.

"Yes, dear, I asked him. That is—" But it was too late. The happiness that had leaped to Dr. Chilton's eyes was unmistakable, and Miss Polly had seen it. With very pink cheeks she turned and left the room hurriedly.

Over in the window the nurse and Dr. Warren were talking earnestly. Dr. Chilton held out both his hands to Pollyanna.

"Little girl, I'm thinking that one of the very gladdest jobs you ever did has been done today," he said in a voice shaken with emotion.

At twilight a wonderfully tremulous, wonderfully different Aunt Polly crept to Pollyanna's bedside. The nurse was at supper. They had the room to themselves.

"Pollyanna, dear, I'm going to tell you—

the very first one of all. Some day I'm going to give Dr. Chilton to you for your—uncle. And it's you that have done it all. Oh, Pollyanna, I'm so—happy! And so—glad!—darling!"

Pollyanna began to clap her hands, but even as she brought her small palms together the first time, she stopped, and held them suspended.

"Aunt Polly, Aunt Polly, *were* you the woman's hand and heart he wanted so long ago? You were—I know you were! And that's what he meant by saying I'd done the gladdest job of all—today. I'm so glad! Why, Aunt Polly, I don't know but I'm so glad that I don't mind—even my legs, now!"

Aunt Polly swallowed a sob.

"Perhaps, some day, dear—" But Aunt Polly did not finish. Aunt Polly did not dare to tell, yet, the great hope that Dr. Chilton had put into her heart.

But she did say this:

"Pollyanna, next week you're going to take a journey. You're going to a great doctor who has a big house many miles from here. He's a dear friend of Dr. Chilton's, and we're going to see what he can do for you!"

A LETTER
FROM POLLYANNA

Dear Aunt Polly and Uncle Tom:

Oh, I can—I can walk! I did today, all the way from my bed to the window! It was six steps. My, how good it was to be on legs again! All the doctors stood around and smiled, and all the nurses stood beside them and cried.

I wanted to sing and shout and yell! Oh, just think, I can walk—walk—walk! Now I don't mind being here almost ten months, and I didn't miss the wedding, anyhow. Wasn't that just like you, Aunt Polly, to come on here and get married right beside my bed, so I could see you. You always do think of the gladdest things!

Pretty soon, they say, I shall go home. I wish I could walk all the way there. I do. I don't think I shall ever want to ride anywhere any more. It will be so good just to walk. Oh, I'm so glad! I'm glad for everything. I'm going to walk eight steps tomorrow.

With heaps of love to everybody,
POLLYANNA.